Books by A MW00943008

McIntyre Security, Inc. Bodyguard Series:

Vulnerable

Fearless

Shane (a novella)

Broken

Shattered

Imperfect

Ruined

Hostage

Redeemed

Marry Me (a novella)

Snowbound (a novella)

Regret

With This Ring (a novella)

Collateral Damage

A Tyler Jamison Novel:

Somebody to Love

Somebody to Hold

A British Billionaire Romance:

Charmed (co-written with Laura Riley)

Audiobooks by April Wilson

For links to my audiobooks, please visit my website:
www.aprilwilsonauthor.com/audiobooks

Shane

McIntyre Security Bodyguard Series
... a novella (book 2.5)

APRIL WILSON

This novel is a work of fiction. All places and locations mentioned in it are used fictitiously. The names of characters and places are figments of the author's imagination. Any resemblance to real people or real places is purely a coincidence.

Wilson Publishing
P.O. Box 292913
Dayton, OH 45429
www.aprilwilsonwrites.com

Visit www.aprilwilsonwrites.com to sign up for the author's e-mail newsletter to be notified about upcoming releases.

ISBN-13: 978-1544184999
ISBN-10: 1544184999

Published in the United States of America
First Printing March 2017

Dedications

To my darling daughter, Chloe.

To my sister and BFF, Lori.

And to all the wonderful people around the world
who read my books. Thank you for making
my dreams come true!

A Night in Jail

Sometimes life grabs you by the balls and squeezes so hard you're in danger of crying uncle. Tonight was one of those nights. One minute, I'm having dinner with the love of my life, enjoying her company, basking in the warmth of her smile and the soft touch of her delicate hand, and the next, I'm sitting on a concrete slab in a Cook County jail cell. My head is pounding, and I've got more than a few bumps and bruises, thanks to Tyler Jamison. But I got in a couple good hits myself tonight. And because of that, I'm sitting here in jail while he goes through the motions of pressing charges against me.

Assaulting an officer. That's pretty ironic, considering the fact he's the one who attacked me. Technically, I should be the one pressing charges.

I take stock of my current situation, which at the moment doesn't look good. I'm in jail, and I've got a lump on the back of my head from where Tyler slammed me into the wall in the foyer of Beth's townhouse. My lip is cut. The knuckles on my right hand are sore and swollen from hitting Tyler back. I guess I shouldn't have done that, but there's only so much a man can take before he has to give a little something back.

My only regret is that Beth saw me hit her brother.

Beth.

Damn it!

My main concern right now is how she's taking all this. I'm not worried about myself. Troy will get me released on bond ASAP. It's Beth I'm concerned about. She's got to be worried sick. It was a traumatic night for her to begin with, seeing Howard Kline in the flesh —in the *dead* flesh—as he lay in a pool of his own blood on her bedroom floor after I put a bullet in his brain. Her big fear all along was that I'd get arrested for shooting Kline. I tried to reassure her there was never any chance of that happening. Jake and I planned this out too well.

I lean my throbbing head against the cold cement wall and close my eyes, trying to slow down the adrenaline that's still coursing through me. I have to keep reminding myself that Beth's all right. She's at home, safe and sound. Cooper's with her, and probably Lia too. They won't leave her side until I get home.

Earlier That Evening

The evening starts out innocently enough. After firing that bitch of a manager, Vanessa Markham, Beth decides to take over as manager of Clancy's Bookshop. I'm glad she made the decision—both to fire Vanessa and to take over as manager herself. She doesn't think she's qualified to take over running the store, but she is.

She'll make a fantastic manager—because she cares. She cares about the employees, about the customers, and about the store itself. That bookstore is her happy place, which is why I bought it for her. Well, for that reason, and because I wanted to impress her. What good is having money if you can't use it to impress the woman you love?

Troy's still giving me hell for buying Clancy's for Beth. But that's his job—as my attorney, he's supposed to tell me when I'm being stupid. But I didn't care then, and I don't regret the decision now. She loves that place, and I love her—and I wanted to score big points with her. She'd needed a little pick-me-up then, and I damn sure wanted to be the one to give it to her.

It's late afternoon when I drive over to Clancy's unannounced and park my car in the VIP spot in front of the building. The first familiar face I see when I walk into the store is Mack Donovan, my hand-picked choice for head of building security. He's standing just inside the front doors, chatting with a uniformed security guard.

"Hey, Mack," I say, as we shake hands.

Mack's name is fitting because the guy's built like a Mack truck. He's huge at six-four, a solid wall of muscle. Brown hair, brown eyes, and a strong, square jaw. He's a fortress. As a former Army Ranger, he's way overqualified for building security, but since this is where Beth spends most of her days, I won't take any chances with her safety. I want the best money can buy. And where Beth is concerned, money is no object. And besides, Mack says he's happy here, so it's a win-win for us both.

"I wasn't expecting you today," Mack says. "To what do we owe the pleasure?"

"I stopped by to surprise Beth and take her out for a celebratory dinner. She told me she fired Vanessa."

Mack nods. "Good riddance to that bitch. Did Beth tell you she's taking over as store manager?"

"She did. Hence the celebration."

I can't help noticing that Mack's gaze keeps darting over to the check-out counter where three terminals are in full swing as cashiers ring out customers. Two of the cashiers are young men whose names I don't know. The third is Erin O'Connor, one of the assistant managers here and now a friend of Beth's. Mack seems to have developed a fascination with the checkout counter, but I don't think it's the men he's eyeing—I know for a fact that Mack doesn't swing that way. That leaves only one other option as the object of his attention.

"Isn't she a little young for you?" I say.

Mack and I are the same age—thirty-four. Beth is ten years younger than I am, and her brother never misses an opportunity to give me grief over the differences in our ages. Tyler thinks I'm too old for his little sister. I disagree, but that's another story. But Mack and Erin? God, Erin's even younger than Beth. Erin's twenty, maybe twenty-one. She's a baby still.

Mack tears his gaze away from little Miss O'Connor and eyes me innocently. "I'm sorry, what was that?"

I shake my head at him. "You heard me. She's too young for you." God, now I sound like Tyler.

Mack frowns, but he doesn't say anything. My guess is, he's been telling himself the exact same thing. I've known Mack for a good while now. He's an honorable guy. "Just be careful, man," I tell him. "She's a sweet kid, and she's Beth's friend." The implied message—*if you hurt Erin, you'll have to deal with me.*

I'm pretty sure he got the message loud and clear because he gives me a look of pure disgust. "You think I don't already know that? *All* of that?"

I nod. Of course he does. Like I said, he's an honorable guy. He'll do the right thing, which is to forget about her.

Mack's gaze shifts, and I glance over to see Erin approaching us, a beaming smile on her face. Her big blue eyes flit over to Mack and for a moment, she sees nothing but him. Her freckled cheeks are flushed, and she's fidgeting nervously in her short boots. Dressed as she is, in a navy skirt, a white blouse buttoned up modestly, a pale blue sweater, with a small gold locket on a gold chain around her neck, she looks like she just stepped out of a parochial high school. God, I feel for poor Mack. She's practically jail bait.

One side of her shoulder-length dark hair is clipped back with a gold barrette. The other side, she pushes back behind her perfect little shell of an ear as she smiles up at Mack.

Finally, she looks at me. "Hi, Shane. I didn't know you were coming today. Beth will be excited to see you."

"I thought I'd surprise her with a dinner date. Do you know where she is?"

Erin nods. "Upstairs in her office, probably still freaking out about taking on the job of general manager. Do you want me to run up and get her?"

"Thanks, but no. I'll go up."

Erin nods, then glances shyly back at Mack. That porcelain complexion of hers is getting pinker by the minute. The girl can't hide a damn thing.

"Well, I guess I'd better get back to work," she says, looking up at Mack, who towers over her.

Mack gives her a cool, friendly smile and nods. "See you later, Erin."

Once she's out of earshot, I look at him. "You have your work cut out for you, my friend. I didn't realize the interest goes both ways."

Mack sighs heavily as he crosses his muscular arms over his equally muscular chest. "I know she's too young," he says, sounding resigned. "And she's too small for me. But knowing that doesn't make this any easier. It's just infatuation. She'll grow out of it as soon as someone else catches her eye.... someone more appropriate. The boys around here trail after her like smitten puppies. It's only a matter of time."

I clap Mack on the shoulder. "Keep telling yourself that, buddy. From where I'm standing, it sure looks like the infatuation goes both ways."

* * *

I walk up the curved marble staircase to the second floor, then head down the private hallway that leads to the administrative offices. I step into the outer office, where a half dozen employees are busy either working at their desks or unpacking shipments of books. The staff glance up at me cautiously, but don't say anything.

I head for the inner door that leads to Beth's office. It's already open, and I peer inside. Beth is seated at her desk, her nose buried in a thick, black binder. Her bodyguard, Sam Harrison, is seated on the ledge of a window overlooking the street, watching something on his phone.

This tattooed punk with the red man-bun and black shitkicker boots is a former Army Ranger, too, like Mack. A parachute malfunction ended Sam's military career, and now he works for me. He's good at what he does. He's also good for Beth.

Sam's gaze immediately snaps to the doorway, and I silently signal for him to vacate the room. Beth is so wrapped up in what she's reading that she doesn't even notice his departure. For a moment I stand in the doorway and observe Beth as she's caught up in her work, allowing myself the pleasure of simply gazing at her.

It amazes me that she has no idea how exquisite she is. Her long blond hair falls in soft waves around an oval face with a peaches-and-cream complexion. I can't see her eyes from this vantage point, but if she looked up, I'd be gazing into a pair of Caribbean blue-green eyes. I swear, I could look at her for hours.

I think back to the first moment I laid eyes on her—right here in this bookstore just five months ago. She was alone, browsing books in the romance section on a Friday evening. I was essentially stalking her—filling in at the last minute for her official covert bodyguard who'd taken ill and ended up in the ER. Seeing her for the first time was like getting hit by lightning. I knew it was a once-in-a-lifetime event.

I don't believe in love at first sight—lust, sure, but not love. And sure, it was lust in the beginning—as soon as I saw her, I wanted her. Badly. But it didn't take long before she stopped being simply a gorgeous woman, and became *Beth*. It didn't take long for me to realize that her heart and her soul were just as beautiful as her face.

And now, she's mine. Well, for all intents and purposes, she's *mine*. I still need to put a ring on her finger and say the vows, but I'm biding my time. It's too soon for that, and I don't want to rush her.

She's naturally cautious, and I don't want to pressure her.

So the diamond engagement ring I spent weeks searching for is safely tucked away in a little velvet box at the back of my sock drawer at home, where it will stay until I think she's ready for it.

I quietly knock on the door jamb, and the moment she glances up at me, a smile lights her face. My heart rate kicks up at the sight of her smile.

"Can I help you, sir?" she says, her soft voice laced with a mixture of amusement and pleasure.

Just hearing her voice makes me hard, and for a moment I entertain the idea of skipping dinner and taking her straight home to bed. But she's in a playful mood, and I can play along. "I'd like to see the manager, please."

"Oh?" Fighting a grin, she leans back in her chair and folds her hands over her belly, looking every bit the professional. "Is there a problem, sir?"

I walk into her office and take a seat on the corner of her desk. "Yes, there's a problem. I was so busy at work today I skipped lunch, and now I'm starving." I reach out to cup her chin, then brush my thumb gently across her cheek. "I'd like to take Clancy's new general manager out to dinner to celebrate her sudden promotion, if she'll let me." *And then I want to take her home and make love with her until she begs for mercy.*

"She'd be delighted, thank you. Where did you have in mind?" she says, sitting forward eagerly.

"I think I'll let the new general manager choose." Honestly, I don't care where we eat. This is just an excuse to take her out on a date.

"You know what I'm craving? How about Sal's Bar-B-Q? Remember, that little barbecue place we ate at in Hyde Park?"

Fuck. Of course I remember the place—we went there on one of our first official dates. It's a five-minute walk from her old townhouse. And that's the last fucking place on Earth I want her to be. Damn it! I guess I just assumed she'd pick somewhere downtown or perhaps in The Gold Coast near our home. I never considered the possibility she'd pick a restaurant in Hyde Park.

Beth has no idea I have a body double living in her old townhouse, in an attempt to make Howard Kline think she's still living there. My brother Jake is overseeing an operation at the townhouse to catch Kline in the act of committing a crime. We're fully expecting him to break in one night, armed, with the intent to kidnap, assault, or even kill Beth. Only it won't be Beth he finds there. It will be one of my best operatives—Caroline Palmer—who could easily pass for Beth's double, and who's well trained in self-defense.

When Kline makes his move, our team will be waiting for him, and we'll take him out once and for all. And since Kline's been busy casing the townhouse lately, getting bolder and bolder with each foray into the neighborhood, Jake's pretty sure he's working up the nerve to carry out his plans. We figure it's just a matter of time.

And Beth had to pick Sal's, just a few blocks away. Damn it, I don't want her anywhere near her old townhouse.

I smile at her, not wanting her to know this is a potential problem. "Sure. That sounds fine," I tell her, mentally kicking myself for not suggesting a restaurant myself in the first place.

* * *

We make our way downstairs to the ground floor, and Beth stops to say goodbye to Sam and Erin and Mack, who are all congregated near the front of the store. Erin's working the check-out counter again, Sam's killing time behind the counter, and Mack's standing a few feet away trying not to hover.

When he sees us coming, Mack meets us at the door and opens it. "Have fun, kids," he says.

I usher Beth outside into the balmy early evening air and open the front passenger door of my Jaguar for her. She slips into her seat, and as I lean in to buckle her seat belt, she rolls her eyes at me. She thinks it's silly for me to do it, but I don't care. I like taking care of her.

"So, sue me," I say, and then I kiss her as I tighten her belt.

As we head south toward our destination, I have to work at reigning in my aversion to the idea of Beth being anywhere near a place frequented by Howard Kline. Jesus! Just the thought of that monster anywhere near her makes my blood boil.

I park on a quiet side street, just a couple blocks from Sal's, and we walk to our destination. I open the vintage wooden door for Beth and follow her inside.

This place probably hasn't changed in half a century. It's like stepping back into an earlier era. I know Beth picked this place because she knows how much I like classic blues music and phenomenal barbecue. Even now, a Muddy Waters classic is playing over the sound system.

I am actually hungry—missing lunch today wasn't a ruse. So the aroma of roasted meats and sweet, tangy barbecue sauce hits me hard.

We grab a booth in the back corner of the restaurant, and Beth slips into the back bench first. I slide in beside her, sharing the same bench rather than sit across the table from her. I don't want a table between us. I want to be able to touch her.

A server brings us two glasses of ice water and takes our drink orders.

The music and the ambiance of this old place speak to me, and for a moment I'm glad we came here. I try to relax and enjoy myself, knowing she picked this place for my benefit. Still, we're just blocks away from Beth's townhouse, and that's just too close for comfort.

Our server brings me a bottle of dark ale and Beth a glass of Coke, and we place our food order. While we're waiting for our food to arrive, I lay my arm across the back of the bench seat, letting my fingers brush lightly against Beth's shoulder, which makes her shiver. But it's not enough contact. I reach for one of her hands and brush my thumb across her knuckles.

She leans into me, laying her head on my shoulder, and she turns her hand in mine so that now she's the one stroking my fingers. She slowly strokes each one, from base to tip, and all I can think about is how good her fingers would feel stroking my dick instead. Just thinking about it makes me hard. She chuckles when I'm forced to shift in my seat to make room for my growing erection.

I have a feeling she knows exactly what she's doing to me. She's starting to realize the effect she has on me. One look, one touch, and she's got my full attention. It's a little embarrassing on my part because no woman has ever had that kind of effect on me. I didn't even know it was possible until I met Beth.

When she starts to massage my hand, pressing the pad of her thumb in firm little circles in the center of my palm, I can't help groaning. I have to shift my position again.

I lean close and whisper in her ear. "You're asking for trouble." She can tease me all she wants in public, but once we get home, it'll be payback time, and she knows it.

With a grin, she releases my hand and slips her arms around my waist, beneath my suit jacket. When her hand accidently brushes against the gun holster strapped to my chest, she flinches and pulls away.

"It's okay," I say, pulling her back into my arms. She's still not used to being around guns—she says they make her nervous. But I never go anywhere unarmed, and it's just something she'll have to get used to. "It's just a precaution. It's nothing to worry about."

Our food arrives, and we dig in, both of us pretty hungry. Beth offers me some of her French fries, and I feed her a few bites of my brisket.

I'm trying to concentrate on finishing my meal, so we can go home, but she's got her hand on my slacks, gently sliding it up and down my thigh. The heat from the slight friction of her hand on my leg warms my skin, and the heat sinks deep inside me. I can feel my dick swelling with each pass of her hand. At this rate, I'm going to have difficulty walking out of this place.

I'm fighting the urge to tell her to eat faster so we can get out of here when my phone chimes with an incoming call. Normally, I would have ignored the call, but this is a distinctive ring tone. I know exactly what it means, and my heart rate automatically picks up. It's Jake.

I pull out my phone and accept the call, skipping the niceties. "Report."

Jake doesn't waste any time. "Kline just boarded a bus for Hyde Park. We think he's armed, dressed in all black, and he's carrying a black duffle bag—something he's never done before. This may be it. We're getting in position."

"God damn it! You're sure?" I've been waiting for this moment for months now. The good news is that I'm just a few blocks away from the townhouse. The bad news—Beth is with me.

"Where's Beth?" Jake says, as if he can read my mind. "She's safe?"

No, she's not fucking safe!

I take a deep breath. "She's here with me. We're at a restaurant in Hyde Park. Fuck! I can't believe the timing."

All Hell Breaks Loose

How soon can we get someone here to pick her up?" I say to Jake. I need Beth out of here. I need someone to collect her and take her back to our penthouse apartment.

"What in the hell is she doing in Hyde Park?" Jake says. "Are you crazy?" He's silent for a moment, and I can just picture him recalculating his strategy. A moment later, he's back on the line. "All right. I'll call Lia, tell her to drop what she's doing and get to your location to pick up Beth. She can be there in thirty minutes. You stay with Beth until Lia arrives."

"No. I can't wait that long, Jake. Damn it! I don't believe this." I glance at Beth, who's listening to my half of the conversation intently, trying to figure out what the hell is going on.

"It's either that," Jake says, "or you have to bring her here, which

I *do not advise.*"

"No, I'm not bringing her," I tell Jake. "It's too risky. I'll call you back."

I end the call, and my mind races as I weigh my options and their inherent risks. I can't take her to the townhouse—that's simply too risky. I have to leave now, there's no question of that. I've got to be at the townhouse—Kline is *my* problem. It's safer for Beth to stay here in the restaurant until someone comes to get her. I shoot off a quick text to Lia, telling her to get her ass over here ASAP. Then I grab my wallet and throw a couple of twenties onto the table to cover our bill.

I turn to Beth. "Listen to me carefully, Beth. Lia's on her way here." I rise to my feet and slip my phone back into my jacket pocket. "She'll take you to the penthouse. Do not move from this table until she gets here."

Beth frowns, and I can see the wheels turning as she pieces everything together. She knows there's no way in hell I'd abandon her like this if it weren't something urgent.

She grabs my wrist. "You're leaving me here? Why? What's wrong?"

Hating the look of disbelief, of *hurt*, on her face, I lean forward and kiss her forehead, willing her to understand that I have good reasons for my actions. When I pull back, I have to force myself to be stern. "You stay right here—don't leave this table, do you hear me? Lia will be here soon. She'll take you home."

As I try to pull away, Beth digs her nails into my wrist. "Where are you going?"

I shake my head, grinding my jaws and hating that I can't tell her the truth. I stiffen my resolve. "Do not leave this table."

I forcibly extricate my wrist from her grip and head toward the exit, but a moment later I hear her quick footfalls as she runs after me.

"Shane!"

I stop and turn, and she careens into me. I grab her shoulders to steady her. "Sit back down and wait for Lia."

"No. This is about Kline, isn't it?"

I have to look away before I blow everything. My heart starts hammering in my chest as my adrenalin kicks into high gear. The clock is ticking—I don't have time for a delay.

"I'm going with you," she says.

"The hell you are!" Everyone in the restaurant is staring at us now, but I couldn't care less. I lean close and lower my voice. "You are not coming with me, Beth. Stay here and do what I said. Don't worry, you'll be perfectly safe until Lia gets here."

She straightens, and I've never seen her look so determined. "If you walk out of here, so will I. You're going to my townhouse, aren't you? Kline's heading there right now, isn't he?"

I close my eyes and count to ten, sighing heavily as I try not to lose my patience with her. "That was Jake on the phone. Kline just boarded a bus headed this way, and he's *armed*. This may be it. This may be our chance—*my* chance—to put a stop to this. I can't miss this opportunity, Beth. I have to be inside your house before he arrives. You need to listen to me and wait here."

Her eyes narrow and I can see she's digging in her heels. This isn't going to go well.

"No. I'm coming with you," she says.

"Damn it, we talked about this!"

"No, *you* talked about it. I want to be there. If something happens—if something goes wrong and you get hurt, I could never live with myself. This isn't your decision to make, Shane. This is my life. It's me he's coming after. I—"

I run my fingers through my hair, frustration getting the best of me. I'm not above begging her. The thought of her being there when this goes down makes my gut sick. "Beth, please don't do this to me."

"I'm not staying here, Shane. I'll follow you."

"Fuck!" I hiss. She's leaving me no choice. I grab her by the arm and propel her toward the exit. "I don't have time to fucking argue with you. Fine, I'll bring you with me, but you will do *exactly* as I say, do you hear me? If not, I swear to God I'll lock you in a closet."

She blanches at my harsh tone, but I can't help it. There's no time to waste, and I don't have time for gentleness. She nearly stumbles as I push her through the open restaurant door and out onto the sidewalk, and I catch her arm to steady her.

* * *

It takes us less than five minutes to get within a block of Beth's townhouse. I park the Jag in the alley behind her street, and we walk the rest of the way. It's getting dark, so I pick up the pace. I call Jake and tell him to meet me at the side door to the garage in two minutes. Just as we arrive at the door, he's there, holding it open and ushering us inside.

Jake takes one look at Beth, then turns to me, scowling. "What the God-damned fuck is *she* doing here?"

I narrow my eyes at him. Yes, I know her presence is a serious complication, but I'm not about to let anyone speak that way in front of her. "Deal with it!" I tell him. "I need to get her somewhere safe."

Jake turns and leads us across the rear yard and into the darkened house through the French doors, which open to the kitchen. Caroline Palmer—Beth's body double—and two other McIntyre Security operatives, Killian Deveraux and Cameron Stewart, both former military special ops, are standing around a table. They all pivot to face us, Killian raising his semi-automatic rifle at us. Just as quickly, Killian lowers his weapon, and they all turn their curious gazes to Beth.

"Change in plans," Jake snaps. "We have a fucking civilian bystander. Where do we put her?"

Killian steps forward. "Put her in—shit! Beth's bedroom is the last room upstairs. He'll look in every upstairs room before he gets to her room. You can't leave her downstairs, so you have no choice but to take her upstairs with you and hide her in her bedroom."

"There's a small walk-in closet in the bedroom," Caroline says. "We can put her in there. It's out of the line of fire, so she should be okay if she hunkers down and has protective gear on."

I glance at Beth's face, which is suddenly as white as a sheet. I don't think she fully realized what she was getting into when she insisted on coming with me. Now that she's here, she doesn't get a say.

Jake shoves a black Kevlar vest into my hands, and I put it on

Beth, adjusting the Velcro straps securely at her shoulders and torso. It's designed for a full-grown man, so it's big on her, but that's fine—it will just cover more of her body. Then Jake hands me one, too, and I strap it on myself.

Jake's phone vibrates, and he peers down at the screen. "ETA bus stop in seven minutes. Everyone into position."

Killian and Cameron slip out the back door and disappear silently into the night. Jake, Caroline, and I head up the back staircase with Beth. On the way up, Jake hands me an earpiece, which I slip into my ear.

Once we reach the upper floor, I walk Beth down the hallway to her bedroom, which is at the far end. She winces at the tight grip I have on her arm, but she doesn't complain.

As soon as we enter her old bedroom, I march her straight into the walk-in closet, following her inside, closing the door partway behind us. I pull the light chain hanging just inside the door, and a single, low-watt bulb flickers on.

We don't have much time.

"You stay in here and don't make a sound, do you hear me?" I tell her. Then I double-check her Kevlar vest to make sure it's strapped securely. Going by her wan expression, I think the seriousness of the situation is finally sinking in. I cradle her face in my hands and pull her close, putting us nose to nose. "Do not make a sound. Do not come out of this closet, no matter what you hear. Do you under-stand me?" I know I sound harsh, but it's necessary.

"Yes," she whispers hoarsely.

I know she's scared, but I don't have time to comfort her. Every second counts now. "There's no time," I say, wishing I could stay here and hold her, chase all her demons away. I wrap my arms around her, despite the bulk of our armored vests. As I kiss the top of her head, I walk her backward into the farthest corner of the closet.

I push her down to the floor into a sitting position, then arrange some clothes that are still hanging on the rod so that they partly obscure her from view. Crouching down in front of her, I grip her chin and make her look me in the eye. "I swear to God, Beth, if you move from this spot, I'll blister your hide, do you hear me? This time I'm not kidding."

She smiles at the reference to a spanking—it's an inside joke for us. When I first met her, she was reading an anthology of spanking stories at Clancy's. I suspect she has a secret spanking fetish.

My thumb brushes over her cheek. "Be safe, Beth." I lean in to kiss her one last time. It's a gentle kiss, the only comfort I have time to give. When I reluctantly pull back, her eyes are glistening with unshed tears.

Now comes the hard part—the part I'm dreading. I hate the idea of leaving her here alone in the dark, but it can't be helped. Thanks to that fucker Kline, she's terrified of the dark. That monster kept her tied up, naked and alone in a freezing cold, pitch-black cellar for almost twelve hours, and to this day she's afraid of the dark. "Now listen to me," I say. "I have to turn off the closet light and shut the door. You will remain frozen in place until I—or one of my people— come to get you. Do you understand?"

"Yes."

Her reply is little more than a croak, and I can tell she's holding back tears.

"You're going to have to be okay here in the dark, sweetheart. I can't let you have any light on. All right?"

She nods. "It's not me I'm worried about." She grabs my wrists. "Be careful."

She's breathing a little too hard now, so I reach inside my Kevlar vest to my jacket pocket and pull out her rescue inhaler and shove it into her hands. "In case you need it."

She swallows hard. "I love you."

Before I can respond, Jake pokes his head into the closet. "ETA two minutes!" he barks in a low voice. "Get into place!"

Then Jake looks at Beth, and as he smiles at her his expression softens.

I brush her cheek. "I love you, sweetheart. Wait here. I'll see you soon."

I back out of the closet, switching off the light as I go, then I gently close the door behind me. I hate knowing she's alone in there, but there's not a damn thing I can do about it at the moment. Not until this is over and Howard Kline is dead.

My priority right now has to be eliminating this monster from Beth's life once and for all.

The Moment of Reckoning

W e're ready. Everyone checks in via the comm system, confirming their locations.

Jake's here in Beth's bedroom with me. Caroline is in the bathroom down the hallway, going through the motions of getting ready for bed. Killian is seated in a parked car down the street, monitoring both the bus stop and the front of the townhouse. Cameron is in the alley behind the townhouse, monitoring the rear of the house. If Kline makes his move, we'll know it.

There's light chatter on the comm system as Jake confers with his people. This is Jake's hand-picked team, and surveillance is his forte, so I let him handle it. I position myself between Beth's bed and the closet, facing the bedroom door, and wait. No matter what happens, I'll stay between Kline and Beth. He won't be getting past me.

I try not to think about Beth right now. I debated giving her an earpiece, too, so she could be kept up to speed on what's happening, but ultimately I decided against it. It's safer for her if she doesn't know what's going on—in case there's a problem.

"Target exited the bus," Killian says, his voice low and steady. The guy has ice in his veins—I don't think I've ever seen him riled up. "He's carrying a black duffle bag. Walking toward the townhouse. Dressed in black, head to toe."

There's a moment of silence over the comm system, then Killian speaks again. "Target cut between two houses to the rear alley. I no longer have visual."

"I've got visual," Cameron says gruffly over the comm. "He's keeping to the shadows, walking toward the townhouse. He's twenty yards from the gate, looking up at the rear of the house."

"Caroline, go," Jake says.

That's Caroline's signal to make like she's getting ready for bed in the upstairs bathroom. The light's on in the bathroom—the only light on in the house—so Kline's attention will be focused there. A moment later, a toilet flushes, then I hear water running from the bathroom faucet. After another few moments, Caroline flips off the bathroom light and heads sedately down the hallway to Beth's bedroom.

"Target has reached the rear gate," Cameron says.

As Caroline steps into the bedroom, she makes eye contact with me, then with Jake, who's standing on the opposite side of the bed. The plan is for Caroline to lie on the bed beneath a quilt to hide the presence of her Kevlar vest and her handgun. Jake and I will flank the bed and cover Caroline, in case Kline does manage to get off a shot. The plan is that he won't. We won't let him get that far.

As she enters the bedroom, Caroline switches off the light, then closes the bedroom door. She climbs into bed and covers herself with the quilt.

Cameron's low voice comes quietly over the comm. "Target is through the gate."

I take a deep breath and close my eyes for a moment, centering myself and willing my heart rate to slow. When this operation goes down, it will happen fast. I need to be focused and centered.

"Target is picking the rear door lock," Cameron says.

Jake turned off the security system earlier, so no alarms will sound.

"He's inside the house," Cameron says. "I'll follow him in."

I glance at Jake just as he turns to face me. Even though the lights are off, there's enough moonlight coming through the sheer white curtains that we can just see each other.

Jake nods to me, then tells his team, "Radio silence."

Everyone's in place. The bedroom door is shut and will stay that way until Kline opens it and walks through. The moment he steps into Beth's bedroom with a loaded gun, he has committed a felony act of aggression, and I am clear to respond accordingly.

The house is so quiet I can hear the ticking of the big grandfather clock downstairs in the front foyer. Soon, the silence is broken by the sound of footsteps on the creaky wooden staircase. A few moments later, I can hear his muffled footfalls on the narrow carpet runner as he slowly makes his way down the hallway. He makes painstakingly slow progress, and I assume he's checking the other two bedrooms and the bathroom first, to make sure there's no one else in the house.

Slowly, the steps continue toward our end of the hallway. There's a moment of silence, then I hear the brass doorknob turn. The mahogany door swings slowly open on squeaky hinges, the sound jarring in the quiet house.

Fading back into the shadows as Kline enters the room, I study him for a split second. I've seen his picture a thousand times, committed his features to memory so there could never be any mistake. Five-foot-ten, two hundred and forty pounds, a balding head, dark eyes that are bloodshot and watery, a flabby face with a sallow complexion and a perpetual five o'clock shadow.

Kline sets his duffle bag on the floor, then pulls a black handgun out of his coat pocket, aiming the muzzle at the bed where Caroline lies perfectly still beneath the quilt. The gun has a silencer. Kline's hand is shaking, and his thick index finger hovers over the trigger. Still, I can see that the safety is on.

His sense of triumph is palpable, and he chuckles as he fixates on the mound beneath the quilt. "You stupid little cunt." His voice is low and hoarse as he points his gun at the bed. "I spent eighteen years in hell because of you! You owe me!"

The thought that this pathetic excuse for a human being thinks Beth owes him anything makes me sick. I feel nothing but revulsion in my gut, and certainly no remorse for what I'm about to do.

My Beretta 9 mm feels solid and familiar in my hand, like an old friend. There's a round in the chamber, and the silencer is on. I'm just waiting for my cue. And Kline gives it to me a moment later when he flips off the safety on his gun. Everything after that happens in a flurry. I step out of the shadows and raise my gun. He turns to face me, startled and confused. His stunned expression would be almost comical if the situation weren't so serious.

Kline opens his mouth, but before he can utter a sound, I fire, hitting him right between the eyes. His wide, unseeing eyes remain locked on me as his knees buckle and he drops to the floor like a stone. His handgun slips from his fingers and strikes the wooden floor with a dull thud.

"He's down!" Jake says. Jake's across the room in a flash, crouching down beside the body to check for a pulse. "The target is down," he says calmly into the comm system. "I repeat, the target is down."

A moment later, Killian and Cameron are in the bedroom with us, one of them flipping on the overhead ceiling light. Caroline sits up, shoving the quilt aside as she climbs out of bed.

I step forward to examine Kline's body myself. There can't be any mistake. There's no detectable pulse, no breath. He's gone. I nod to my brother. "He's dead, Jake. Make the call."

I remove my Kevlar vest and head straight for the closet door, slowly opening it. "Beth, honey, it's me. I'm coming in."

Beth raises her hands to shield her tear-filled eyes from the bright light. I holster my gun as I scan her quickly to make sure she's all right. Then I step inside and close the door partway behind me to block some of the light. "It's done, sweetheart. It's over."

Beth clambers to her feet and rushes into my arms, shaking, her face wet with tears. She's still holding the rescue inhaler I'd left with her, and I take it from her trembling hand and stow it in my jacket pocket.

Feeling overwhelmed with relief that Kline is dead and Beth is safe, I squeeze her tightly in my arms. "It's all right now," I murmur into her hair. "Everything's all right."

"Was that Kline?" she says. "Is he dead?"

I nod as I remove her armored vest. "He's dead. He'll never threaten you again."

Beth glances up at me, studying me. "Is everything okay?"

Everything's fine. But right now I just want to get Beth downstairs and away from Kline's body. I don't want her to see the corpse lying on her old bedroom floor, or the pool of blood that's spreading out from beneath his head. And I certainly don't want her to see the hole I put dead center of his forehead.

I wrap my arm around her, hoping to steer her directly out of the closet and out the bedroom door. "Fine. I'm going to take you downstairs now. You can wait with me until the police arrive."

But unfortunately, Beth has other plans. "I want to see Kline," she says. "I want to see his body."

She starts for the closet door, but I stop her. "Beth, there's no need–"

"I need to see his body. I need to see with my own eyes that he's dead."

"Beth–"

She brushes past me, determined to do this, but stops abruptly as she steps into the bedroom. Just a few feet from the closet is where Kline's body lies on the floor, a dark pool of blood staining the wooden floors beneath him.

Beth glances at Jake, who's standing guard over the body. Then she looks down at Kline's face and shudders. She steps closer, her eyes going to the widening pool of blood. When she sees Kline's discarded gun on the floor, she stiffens.

"He could have been a free man," she says in a quiet voice. "He could have just walked away."

I gently place my hands on her arms and pull her back against my chest. "He made his choice," I say. "Now let's go downstairs and wait for the police. You don't need to see this."

Beth shudders at the mention of the police.

"Don't worry," I tell her. "Everything's going to be fine." As I'm stroking her arms in an attempt to comfort her, I realize she's crying. "Please don't cry." I can't bear it when she cries. When her tears turn into sobs, I quietly lead her out of the bedroom and down the stairs.

The Authorities

I escort Beth downstairs to the front parlor and sit her down on the sofa. She hasn't said a word, and I'm pretty sure she's in shock. I'm trying to play it calm and cool, hoping to reassure her. But the truth is, anything can happen at this point. Jake called 911. Now we wait for the cops to show up and process the scene.

I put my arm around Beth and draw her close. She leans into me and takes hold of my hand, clutching it tightly in her lap. I kiss the top of her head. "It'll be all right, sweetheart. Don't worry." God, I hope that's the case. If this goes south, Beth will be devastated.

Cooper lets himself in through the front door with his key and pauses in the foyer. We exchange glances through the open foyer door, then he looks up the staircase, trying to make sense of the muffled voices coming from upstairs.

He glances back at me, his expression somber. "Do you want me to call Troy?"

I shake my head, not willing to admit I might need my attorney to bail me out. "Not yet. Let's see how this plays out. If there's a complication, call him."

A complication? In other words, if I find myself under arrest. But I hope it doesn't come to that. I promised Beth it wouldn't.

Beth makes a pained sound, and I tighten my hold on her, pressing my lips to her hair. "Relax, honey."

"Don't worry, Beth," Cooper says from the foyer. He peers through one of the sidelites beside the big mahogany front door as he watches for the cops to arrive. "What Shane did is perfectly lawful," he continues. "Kline committed a felony by breaking into your home. Armed. Shane faced the threat of imminent death or great bodily injury. He's in the clear. They'll question him, but they won't arrest him."

The front of the house is lit up suddenly with flashing lights from multiple patrol cars. I take a deep breath and steel myself for whatever's about to come next. Whatever it is, I'll do my best to shield Beth from the fallout.

Cooper looks at me. "Shane, they're here."

I kiss Beth's temple, then rise from the sofa. "Cooper, come sit with Beth." I don't want her to be alone in this.

I walk to the foyer as Cooper opens the front door and admits three uniformed police officers. One of the officers has his hand on the butt of his gun.

"Hello, officers," I say in greeting, my voice low.

"We have reports of a deceased individual at this address," one of them says, his gaze sweeping the foyer and front room.

I nod. "Upstairs, in the back bedroom. An armed male broke into my girlfriend's home and entered her bedroom. His name is Howard Kline. He's a convicted felon. He walked into Beth's bedroom and pointed a gun at her bed. I shot him before he could fire a shot. My brother's up there now with the body."

One of the officers races up the stairs, while the other two start taking down my statement and making notes. Out of the corner of my eye, I watch as Cooper puts his arm around Beth, probably in an attempt to keep her from coming over here. My darling girl can be rather persistent.

I answer all their initial questions... giving them my name, address, occupation, my relationship with Beth, and so forth. Just the basics, it's pretty much standard procedure. So far, so good. If we can get through all of this without any hitches, there's a chance I'll be able to take Beth home to our apartment soon.

I'm in the middle of answering some final questions when I see a black pick-up truck pull to an erratic stop at the curb in front of the townhouse. *Shit*. Well, here's our complication. I'd recognize that truck anywhere.

Tyler Jamison, Beth's older brother—her very *protective* older brother who just happens to be a Chicago homicide detective—jumps out of the truck and races up the front walk and in through the open door.

The cops wave Tyler in—obviously, they know him.

Tyler must have been off duty, as he's dressed in sweats and a police department T-shirt. His detective's badge is pinned to the waist-band of his sweats. How in the hell did he hear about the shooting so fast?

Tyler wastes no time getting right in my face. "Is she here? Where is she?"

I tip my head in Beth's direction, even as I'm still answering the patrol officer's questions.

Tyler assesses Beth with a quick glance, assuring himself she's un-harmed, then he lunges at me with no warning, grabbing me by the front of my shirt and slamming me hard into the foyer wall, hard enough to make my head bounce off the hard plaster.

"What the fuck were you thinking?" he growls, grimacing at me as he wraps his hands around my throat and squeezes, effectively cutting off my air. His face is flushed, and every muscle in his body is taut as he holds me pinned to the wall. "You God damned son of a bitch! She could have been killed!"

I keep my gaze focused on Tyler until I hear Beth's frantic voice.

"Tyler, stop!" she yells.

My gaze shoots to her just as Cooper grabs her and hauls her back down beside him on the sofa, wrapping his arms around her and holding her there.

I grab Tyler's wrists and pry them off my throat. Tyler pulls free and slams his fist into my face, knocking my head back into the wall, hard enough to crack the plaster. Beth is screaming in the back-ground as I shake my head in an attempt to clear my vision. I can feel warm blood streaming from my nose and down my chin. Furious, I channel all my frustration into Tyler, charging into him and pushing him across the hall into the opposite wall. I drive my fist into his abdomen, knocking the breath out of him, and he doubles over, gasping. I catch him in the face with a sharp blow from my elbow, snapping his head back.

As we're grappling with each other, both of us manage to get in a few good blows before the two cops jump into the fray, hauling me off Tyler. The bigger of the two officers slams me face first into the wall, his hand around the back of my neck to hold me in place while the other officer grabs my right arm and wrenches it up high behind my back. I feel the cold, heavy metal of a handcuff tightening on my right wrist. My chest is heaving, and I have to lean into the wall for support as the cop brings up my other wrist and locks it in the cuff.

Heavy footsteps come pounding down the wooden staircase, and I glance up to see Jake.

"Fuck," he says, looking first at me, then at Tyler, who's still trying to catch his breath.

"Stay with the body!" I tell Jake, who nods curtly and heads back up the stairs.

Tyler's face is flushed as he glares at me. "What the fuck were you thinking, Shane?"

I know I have to be a bloody mess. My bottom lip is throbbing, and I can taste blood in my mouth. Tyler doesn't look so hot either. His nose is bleeding profusely now, and there's blood at the corner of his mouth.

"I did what had to be done," I hiss at him through clenched teeth.

Beth careens into my side, nearly knocking me off balance, and grabs one of my arms. Her eyes are swimming in tears.

One of the officers grabs Beth and tries to pry her off me. "Miss –"

"Get her back, Cooper!" I shout, my voice hoarse.

Tyler's across the foyer, leaning against the wall. "Arrest him," he says to the officers.

Shit, this is going south quickly.

The officer holding me against the wall starts reading me my rights. "You have the right to remain silent," he says. "Anything you say can and will be used against you in a court of law."

"No!" Beth cries. She looks frantic, and she's breathing fast—too fast. She's heading right into an asthma attack. Cooper catches her just as she starts swaying.

"Get her inhaler!" I tell him. "It's in my jacket pocket."

Tyler beats him to it, reaching inside my jacket to pull out Beth's inhaler. He shakes it and puts it to her mouth. "Breathe in, Beth," he says, as he administers the medication. "It's okay, kiddo. Just breathe."

This is all my fault. I never wanted this to happen—I never wanted her to see anything like this. "Beth—Jesus, sweetheart, I'm sorry."

Beth turns to face her brother, and she looks devastated. "Tyler, please. Don't let them take him."

Tyler looks away, avoiding both Beth's gaze and mine. "Take him to the local precinct," he tells the officers. "I'll be along shortly, after I see to my sister."

"On what charges?" she demands.

"Assaulting a police officer," Tyler says, looking belligerent.

Tyler walks Beth into the parlor, and he sits down beside her on the sofa. She tries to lunge to her feet, but Tyler catches her and makes her sit back down beside him. "Sit down, Beth, before you fall down."

I have to crane my head back to see her. "Don't worry, sweetheart. Everything will be fine," I say, trying my best to sound confident. Then I turn to Cooper. "I guess you'd better call Troy."

The two officers march me out to one of the patrol cars. The situation is unreal, strobe lights flashing brightly, lighting up half the neighborhood, bathing the front of the townhouse in bursts of light. I notice more than a few neighbors venturing out of their homes to watch.

When we reach the patrol car, one of the officers pushes me against the side of the vehicle and holds me there by my arm while the other one searches me, systematically patting me down from shoulder to ankle, confiscating my wallet, the Beretta and extra clip from my chest holster, my phone, and the small knife I've got hidden in a calf holster beneath my slacks.

While the officer is frisking me, I glance back to see Beth watching from the front window, looking absolutely heartbroken. Tyler stands behind her, his hands on her shoulders.

I don't think the guy realizes the damage he's done to his sister.

Hauled Off Like a Common Criminal

I've gotten in trouble with the law before—but not since I was a teenager and got pulled over for drag racing with my brothers out in the country. But even then, I got off with a stern warning. I've never been handcuffed in the back seat of a squad car before.

It's impossible to get comfortable in the rear seat of a police cruiser—they're designed for containment, not for aesthetics. My arms are wrenched behind my back, my wrists cuffed, making the seating arrangements challenging.

The charge against me is bogus, of course. Tyler came at me first, and there are plenty of witnesses. I was just defending myself. That will be easy to argue in court, should it come to that, but I'm hoping it won't. I'm hoping Tyler will come to his senses sooner rather than later.

I just have to be patient and go through the motions until Tyler feels like he's gotten his pound of flesh. The problem is, I don't know if Tyler will try to replace the assault charge with something a little more serious—something a little harder to shake—like manslaughter, or even homicide. But I honestly can't believe he'd do something like that to Beth—surely he realizes she'd never forgive him. Besides, Tyler wanted Kline permanently out of the picture just as much as I did.

I can't stop thinking about Beth and what she's going through right now. She's got to be absolutely terrified. First, seeing Kline's dead body in her old bedroom, and then seeing Tyler and me going at it. Cooper will take her back to our penthouse, and he'll stay with her until I get home. I know she's in good hands, but I hate not being the one to comfort her. I could wring Tyler's neck for doing this. In his blinding rage at me, he's not thinking straight.

We arrive at the precinct, and the arresting officer opens the rear door for me and I duck my head as I awkwardly climb out of the car. He walks me through a side entrance, directing me to the booking room to the right, where I'm instructed to remove my Rolex, belt, and shoes, which are confiscated along with the rest of my personal property. Then I'm patted down by the arresting officer once more, and all my pockets are checked for contraband.

Because I look like a wreck, the arresting officer takes me to a medical clinic, where a nurse cleans the drying blood off my face and examines the damage. Since they are only superficial injuries, the booking process continues.

After I'm booked, fingerprinted, photographed, and interviewed, the arresting officer directs me into a small, square holding cell and locks the door behind me. Now comes the hard part—waiting. Waiting for my attorney, Troy, to show up. Waiting for Tyler to show his cowardly face—because, yeah, he'll definitely come, if just to gloat over me.

My holding cell is about 10 by 10, with a concrete slab bench that I suppose functions as both a seat and a bed. There's a gray vinyl pad on it providing a meager bit of padding. There's no blanket, no pillow. The only other fixtures in the barren room are a stainless steel toilet and sink combo, and a surveillance camera embedded in the wall.

I take a seat on the padded bench and lean my head back against the cold, cement wall and close my eyes. My head is pounding from the knocks it took back at the townhouse, and it's bright in here, which doesn't help my headache any. It's relatively quiet, though, which is a blessing. There aren't many holding cells in this small neighborhood precinct.

I keep seeing the stricken look on Beth's face as she watched the officer frisking me. God, I'd give anything to be with her right now. I'd wrap her in my arms and hold her as long as it took to stop her shaking. I'd carry her to our bed and lie quietly with her, holding her in my arms to reassure her.

Instead, I'm here, and she's halfway across the city.

* * *

A couple hours later, my head is still throbbing, and I'm frustrated out of my mind and anxious about Beth when I hear two voices arguing loudly down the hall. It's not difficult to make out the voices of Tyler and my attorney. A third voice, deeper than the other two, jumps into the fray—my brother Jake. It sounds like there's a party going on down the hall in my honor, but I wasn't invited.

A few moments later, Troy appears at my holding cell door, looking exasperated and slightly out of breath. His normally well-groomed head of dark hair is a tousled mess. He's dressed in jeans and a sweatshirt, and holding a black leather briefcase. A moment later, he's joined by an equally irritated uniformed officer.

I meet Troy at the door to my cell, grabbing hold of the bars like I'm in some second-rate prison flick. "Tell me I'm being released."

Troy nods. "Be patient. I'm working on getting bond set for you so I can get you released." His eyes narrow as he looks me over. "You look like shit. Are you okay? Do you need medical attention? I can get you moved to a hospital if need be."

I reach around to gently examine the lump on the back of my head, glad to see that it's gone down a little. "I'll live. Just get me out of here, will you? I need to be home with Beth, not spinning my wheels in here."

He nods. "I'm on it. Sit tight."

As soon as Troy and the uniformed officer leave, Tyler appears at my cell door, his expression strained. He looks nothing like the carefully-controlled man I know him to be. I doubt he's ever lost control like he did tonight. His face is bruised and there's a bandage across the bridge of his nose. His arms are crossed over his chest and he's glaring at me. He seems really shaken, and it takes the edge off my anger.

I sigh, keeping my voice low. "She was *never* in any real danger, Tyler. I would never have let her get hurt. Surely you know that."

He leans closer and speaks in a low voice, practically gritting his teeth. "She was in the *same room* with a convicted felon, Shane! One who wanted to hurt her!"

I shake my head. "I had her in a safe location. She was wearing body armor, and there were *three* of us—armed—in the room with Kline. There was no way in hell he could have gotten to her. I didn't want her there in the first place, but that's just how it went down. When Beth realized Kline was on his way to her townhouse, she insisted on coming with me. Keeping her with me was far safer than leaving her behind, hoping she'd obey me and stay put until someone arrived to collect her. Your sister has a stubborn streak, in case you haven't noticed."

Tyler's lips twitch slightly as if he's fighting a smile. Still, he's not ready to make nice. "You should never have taken her there in the first place."

"I know, but she really didn't give me any choice." I clench my jaws, losing patience with Tyler's accusations. "I had the situation under control, Tyler, and she was never in any real danger. By keeping me here, you're only hurting Beth. Is that really what you want?"

Tyler shifts uncomfortably on his feet. He has to realize what my arrest is doing to Beth. Wordlessly, he turns and walks away.

In frustration, I slam my palms against the bars, then begin pacing the small barren room.

* * *

After half an hour of pacing, I pause when I hear footsteps coming down the hallway toward me. A moment later, Troy Spencer and the arresting officer appear at my cell door. Troy steps back as the officer unlocks the door and lets it swing wide open.

"You're a free man," Troy says. "Tyler dropped the charges. Come collect your personal property and I'll walk you out. Jake's waiting out front to drive you home."

I follow the officer to the booking desk and wait for him to hand me a sealed bag containing my personal belongings. I quickly sign for my stuff, anxious to get home.

"Let's get out of here," I say to Troy, then head for the exit.

Outside, Jake is seated behind the wheel of his SUV, the engine running. I climb into the front passenger seat and close the door.

Troy stands at my open window. "You think you should stop by the hospital and get your head looked at?" he says.

"No, I'm going home."

Troy nods. "All right. Go get some rest. Call me if anything else comes up."

A Free Man

Now that I'm a free man, the only thing on my mind is getting home to Beth. Jake doesn't even bother to ask me—he just heads for my apartment building after informing me that he's already had someone collect my Jaguar. I'd call ahead and let Beth know I'm on my way, but it's the middle of the night, and if she's sleeping, I don't want to wake her.

"You okay?" Jake says as he picks up speed on Lake Shore Drive.

I roll down my window to let in the fresh air, needing it to blow away the stink I feel from having spent half the night cooling my heels in a holding cell. I feel numb. Everything happened so quickly this evening... Kline, Tyler's temper tantrum. Damn it, he and I need to come to an understanding quick. We can't keep doing this to Beth.

I feel the back of my head, relieved to find the knot is shrinking. "Yeah, I'm okay."

I check the time. It's three-thirty am. I just hope Beth was able to sleep.

"I've been keeping tabs on Beth," Jake says as if reading my mind. "She's okay. She's sleeping. Sophie and Liam stopped by to check on her. Lia's been there with her all evening. Cooper, too. She had a lot of support tonight."

I nod, grateful to my family and Cooper. Once we arrive, Jake parks in the underground garage and we head straight up in the express elevator. Just moments later, I'm walking through the foyer doors into the great room, and my heart is pounding with anticipation of seeing Beth. It's dark and silent, and there's a faint glow of embers coming from the hearth. The only other source of light is the ambient city night lights coming through the full-length windows.

Cooper's sitting in an armchair near the fireplace, facing the arched doorway. He regards me calmly.

I make a beeline for the sofa that faces the fireplace and lean over the back of it to find two blond-haired bodies huddled beneath opposite ends of a blanket. One of those blond heads has to be Beth's. I figure out which one it is, then I lean down and kiss her gently on the forehead.

Beth stirs and turns to look up at me, her eyes squinting in the dark. "Shane?"

"Yeah." I'm surprised at how hoarse my voice is. I lean closer, anxious to get my arms around her. "I'm home, just a little worse for wear."

She wraps her arms around my neck and pulls me down for a proper kiss.

I attempt to pull back with a laugh. "I'm also a little ripe, honey. I need a shower."

"Don't care," she says, using one of my lines, and then she pulls me close for another kiss.

I pull back the blanket and scoop her up in my arms, lifting her to my chest.

"For crying out loud, can you guys keep it down?" Lia mutters, pulling the blanket over her head. "I'm trying to sleep here. Jesus, it's like Grand Central Station."

"Nice to see you, too," I say to my little sister. I'm glad she was here tonight for Beth. I'm glad they've grown so close. They're good for each other. I reach down to mess up her hair through the blanket—something I know she hates.

She slaps my hand away. "Cut it out, will ya? Princess has been a basket case all night. Take her to bed, pal."

Lia burrows beneath her blanket, and I figure she's sleeping here for the night. I turn to look at Cooper, nodding in appreciation. He returns the gesture, then rises to his feet and heads down the hallway to his own suite.

* * *

God, it feels good to be home, good to have Beth in my arms, and good to know that Kline is no longer a threat. Not to Beth, not to anyone. He's gone. *He's dead.* I keep reminding myself of that fact, and each time I feel a surge of satisfaction knowing I was the one to remove this monster from her life. She's safe from him now. It's going to take some time before that really sinks in for both of us.

Beth's only half awake, warm and drowsy in my arms, and a little in shock still, I think. She's going to need time to process what happened tonight... not just Kline actually breaking into her townhouse with the intention of *hurting* her, but Tyler's reaction afterward, seeing the two of us fighting, and then Tyler having me arrested out of spite.

Beth loves her brother—I get that. And I'd never stand between them. But Tyler's very territorial when it comes to his sister. It's going to take time for him to loosen the reigns and accept me as Beth's lover.

Once we're in our suite, I close the door behind us and lay Beth gently on her side of our big bed. It's late—or rather it's very early. We both need sleep, desperately, but I have to have a shower. I reek.

Beth's already dressed for bed, so I leave her tucked beneath the bedding and head to the bathroom for a quick shower. After a brisk scrub, I towel myself off and head straight to bed, climbing in naked and a little damp beside her.

Sighing, I pull her into my arms and hold her. God, I want her right now—I'd give anything to sink into her sweet, tight warmth—but she needs sleep more than she needs sex.

Beth turns to me and presses her face against my bare chest, and the feel of her lips against my skin sends a tingle down my spine to my balls.

"Tell me," she says drowsily, her voice little more than a sigh.

"Tyler dropped the charges." I frown when she flinches. I know she feels responsible for Tyler's actions, which of course is ridiculous.

"You should never have been charged in the first place. He assaulted you. I'm so sorry, Shane."

I tighten my hold on her, trying to figure out what to say to lighten her load. "It's not your fault, sweetheart. Tyler had a right to be pissed at me—I should never have let you come with me last night. But, short of handcuffing you to the table at Sal's, I really didn't have much choice."

She chuckles and relaxes into my arms.

"This is between me and your brother, Beth. He and I need to come to terms with each other. We're both stubborn, and we both have a claim on you. It's just that my claim trumps his now, and he hates that."

"He's my brother, Shane. I love him."

"Of course you love him," I say. I don't want her to feel like she has to choose between us. It's not an either-or situation. Tyler and I just need to learn how to work together—how to *trust* each other—for Beth's sake. I kiss her forehead. "Don't worry, sweetheart. Since he and I both love you, and neither one of us appears to be willing to give you up, we'll just have to learn to get along. It would help, though, if he'd stop trying to strangle me."

Her body vibrates with quiet laughter, but she quickly sobers. "Is the danger passed, then?" she says. "There won't be any more charges? Of any kind?"

"There's an ongoing investigation, but that's routine. It's nothing to worry about. What I did was justified self-defense. Now close your eyes and try to relax. I just want to hold you and sleep for a week."

I coax Beth to turn over, facing away from me, so I can spoon behind her. This is our favorite sleeping position, my arm tucked around her waist, our legs intertwined. I press my face into her hair and breathe in her familiar, delectable scent. As I kiss the back of her head and murmur quietly to her, her muscles loosen and she relaxes into sleep.

But sleep doesn't come quite so easily for me. There's still an adrenalin overload in my system, and my pulse is still pretty fast. Every time I close my eyes, I see a replay of the take down in my mind—a typical reaction to any tense operation .... the bedroom door opening, Kline walking in the room, his eyes glued to the bed, pulling his gun and pointing it at someone he thinks is Beth. Mentally, I go through the motions over and over, lifting my own gun, aiming, firing. I relive those few seconds over and over in my head, drawing it out slowly in my memories.

I try hard not to go down the *what-if* rabbit hole. What if I had missed? What if Kline had managed to get off a shot? What if he'd hit Caroline? Dear God, what if Kline had realized the true object of his obsession was hiding in the closet? I physically shudder at the thought.

Beth whimpers in her sleep, and I wonder if she's picking up subconsciously on my agitation. My hands start shaking and I'm forced to pull away from her because I don't want to wake her up. It's a delayed reaction to violence—something I'm very familiar with from my days in the military. It'll take a while to subside.

Carefully, I leave our bed and head across the suite to the bar and pour myself a shot of Glen Livet. Sitting on the sofa, I knock back the whisky, savoring the liquor as it burns a path down my throat and settles in my empty belly, warming me. I pour a second shot and sip this one slowly as I watch Beth sleeping across the room. I think it'll be a while before I can take my eyes off her.

The whisky helps, and I return to bed. With my arm wrapped securely around Beth's waist, I'm finally able to close my eyes and relax for the first time in nearly twelve hours.

A New Day

Something rouses me from my sleep and I open my eyes to see Beth watching me. Her cheeks are flushed pink and her pupils are dilated. She's staring at my mouth, and that makes me smile.

"Good morning," I say, surprised at how rough my voice sounds. I think I could easily use about ten more hours of sleep. I reach out and slide the tips of my fingers across her cheek.

"Good morning," she says back. "You slept a long time." Beth reaches up and touches my face, brushing the pad of her thumb along my lower lip.

I can't resist kissing it. "It was a long night last night. How are you holding up? I was worried about you." That's an understatement.

"That should be my line," she says. "I was worried about *you*."

I chuckle. "Honey, I pay Troy good money to keep me out of trouble. There was never anything to worry about. I just had to wait out Tyler's little temper tantrum."

She laughs at that, just as I had hoped. "It's eight-thirty," she says. "We'll both be late for work."

I shake my head. There's no way in hell I'm letting her out of my sight—not for several days at least. "We're not going to work today—neither of us. We're going to play hooky and spend the day together."

She gives me a huge smile.

I lean forward and kiss her. "So, what do you want to do today? You name it, we'll do it."

Her eyes light up. "Can we go to the lake? I've hardly spent any time there all summer."

I smile. A leisurely day spent at the lake sounds wonderful. "Absolutely." I kiss her again before sitting up in bed. "Let's get cleaned up and dressed, then we'll have some breakfast. After that, we'll walk down to the beach and play tourist all afternoon."

I call my executive assistant, Diane, to tell her I won't be in today and ask her to reschedule my appointments. Beth sends her assistant manager a similar message and asks her to take over as acting general manager for the day. Then she sends text messages to both Lia and Sam telling them they have the day off.

* * *

Not surprisingly, we end up in the shower together. I've told myself *no sex*, to give Beth a little space, but we still end up with our hands all over each other in the shower. It was probably inevitable. There's something about naked, wet bodies and soapy hands that makes it a foregone conclusion that we have to touch each other.

At first, it's just fun, but before I know it, we're kissing beneath the spray of water. My dick is hard as a rock, begging for attention, but when she reaches for it, I grab her hands and distract her with more kisses. *No sex!*

When we're both fairly waterlogged, we step out of the shower to dry off. With a towel wrapped around my waist, I sit on a wooden bench in the bathroom and watch Beth go about her morning routine, applying deodorant and lotion and a tiny bit of mascara. I watch her comb her wet hair, then blow it dry. Finally, we both brush our teeth, standing side-by-side at the same sink. There's something very soothing and reassuring about sharing a bathroom with her... watching her go through her morning routine.

Once out of the bathroom, Beth slips on her undergarments, then dons a pair of shorts and a short-sleeved shirt. Since we're going casual today, I pull on a pair of cargo shorts, a T-shirt, and sneakers.

Walking into the kitchen, we find Cooper seated at the breakfast bar drinking coffee and reading a book on his tablet.

"It's about time," he says, setting down his cup. "I was about to send out a search party." Cooper points to the plates of food warming on the stove. "There's your breakfast."

I pat him on the shoulder. "Thanks, man."

No matter how many times I've told him he's not here to cook for us, or wait on us, he can't help himself. He's a natural born caretaker at heart. He loves to cook. He loves to fuss over Beth. I wish the guy would settle down with someone because he'd make a fantastic partner—if only he'd just let loose and allow it to happen.

Beth and I take our usual seats at the breakfast bar to enjoy our hot food and coffee. Cooper made pancakes this morning—Beth's favorite.

After finishing her breakfast, Beth gets up and hugs Cooper fiercely. "Thank you, Cooper. For last night and for breakfast. For everything. I love you."

Cooper blushes at her open show of affection and eyes me over the top of Beth's head, smiling sheepishly. Beth and Cooper have developed a special bond, for which I'm grateful. Beth's own father died in the line of duty as a Chicago police officer when she was just an infant. And Cooper has no close family. He's never been married and has no children. I think he and Beth naturally gravitated toward each other. She needs a father, and he needs a family. They hit it off right from the start. I'm happy because it means there's one more person to love and watch over Beth—and Cooper makes an excellent protector.

"You're welcome, kiddo," Cooper says to Beth, patting her back. "Let's just hope Shane doesn't make a habit of spending the night in jail."

* * *

I follow Beth back to our suite. As she finishes getting ready for our outing, I strap on my gun holster and Beretta, then pull on a blue plaid shirt to conceal the gun. Kline may no longer be in the picture, but I'm not going out unarmed.

When Beth disappears into the bathroom, I pull a small, black velvet ring box out from the back of my sock drawer, where it's been hiding for days now. I know it's too soon to give it to her, but after last night, I feel a burning desire to get that ring on her finger.

I feel like I've known Beth all my life, but the truth is, it's only been about five months. I know that's not long enough for someone to make a life-long decision about how she wants to spend the rest of her life—and with whom—but my mind is made up. I'm going to be her husband. I'm going to love, honor, and cherish her for the rest of her life—if she'll have me. I know she loves me, I don't doubt that. But whether or not she's ready to make a commitment is another story.

I open the lid of the ring box and stare at its contents—a delicate gold band with a vintage diamond setting—and ponder my plan of attack. I could ask her outright to marry me, but there's a risk she might say no simply because it's too soon. I get that. But that's a risk I'm not willing to take. The alternative is to offer it to her as some kind of promise ring, but that doesn't sit well with me either—I know I want a commitment with her. A promise ring seems too ambiguous.

I carry the ring over to one of the full-length windows and study it in the bright morning light. The diamond is flawless, beautifully cut, with perfect bezels reflecting clear bright light. It's not a big diamond—just shy of a full carat, certainly not as big as what I would have liked to get her. But I know Beth. She wouldn't want a big, ostentatious display of wealth. She'd much prefer a smaller, more modest diamond. It's a beautiful ring, no doubt, and it's more in fitting with her taste. I did my best to choose a ring she would have chosen for herself.

Before I can come to any decision, she breezes out of the bathroom, looking radiantly happy. Her hair is up in a ponytail, which makes her look impossibly young, and my heart tightens painfully in my chest. As she's preoccupied picking up the clothing we left on the floor last night and depositing it into the laundry hamper, I discretely close the ring box and slip it into the oversized pocket of my cargo shorts.

* * *

The beach is just a few hundred yards from our apartment building, so we walk, enjoying the sunshine and fresh air. It's a perfect day for a stroll along Lake Michigan. We reach Oak Beach just minutes later and of course, it's packed with both tourists and locals enjoying this mild, late summer day. So we head north along the wide, paved pathway and follow Lakeshore Trail as it hugs the shoreline.

As always, the path is bustling with bikers, joggers, power walkers, parents pushing baby strollers and chasing after toddlers. We take our time, strolling hand-in-hand. The skies are clear, and we can see well out into the lake where the yachts cruise and ski jets race across the waves.

When we reach North Avenue Beach, we stop for iced coffee drinks at a cafe. Beth takes off her sandals and wades into the surf, standing knee-deep in water that I know is chilly as hell.

"Come sit down with me for a bit," I say as she approaches. I take her hand and lead her to a wooden park bench beneath a large shade tree not far from the beach. We sit there for a while, my arm across her shoulders. She pulls my free hand into her lap and links our fingers together. After the chaos of last night, it's a pleasure to be able to simply relax with her.

I watch the young families strolling by and try to picture myself in the role of husband and father. I'm not afraid of commitment, but I've never felt the need to make one with a particular woman before. But when I do think of taking that step, Beth is the only woman I can picture myself taking it with. And when I think of her being married someday, maybe becoming a mother, I know it has to be with me. I can't picture my life without her in it.

I'm going to do it. Maybe I'm rushing things. And maybe it's unfair to spring this on her after last night's drama. But my instincts are screaming at me to do it. I'm going to offer her the ring and pray she accepts it.

My heart is racing. "I have something for you," I say, still not sure what exactly I'm going to say to her.

She glances up at me, a curious expression on her face. "Oh? What is it?"

I'm flying by the seat of my pants here, but my gut says go for it. I reach into my pocket and withdraw the ring box and hold it out to her. She reaches for it, and I wrap my hands around hers, holding them as I study her gaze for the slightest clue as to what she's thinking. I feel the slightest tremor in her hands.

I honestly don't know what to say. I could always go with the truth, which is "*I know I'm jumping the gun here, Beth, but I don't give a damn. I want you to marry me, so say yes. I don't care that it's too soon. I'm sorry if you're not ready for this.*" But of course I can't say any of that, so I just say the one thing I know deep in my heart. "I love you, Beth." Then I release her hands. "Go ahead. Open it." Damn it, I don't think I've ever been so nervous in my life.

Beth opens the little black box and stares with wide eyes at its contents. For a long, agonizing moment, she says nothing. My heart is in my throat as I watch her expression for a clue to what she's thinking. I honestly don't know what I'll do if she rejects it.

"It's beautiful." Her voice is little more than a sigh. She looks up at me, her blue-green eyes wary. "What is this?"

I smile, realizing she really doesn't know. Then it comes to me. I know what I'm going to say—I'm just going to be honest with her and put it out there for her to decide what she's ready for. "It's whatever you want it to be, sweetheart. Whatever you're ready for. A friendship ring, a promise ring. *An engagement ring.* You tell me."

She glances down at the ring cradled in her hands and her eyes fill with tears.

Damn it! I should have waited. I lift her chin so that we're looking eye to eye, then lean forward and kiss her gently on the lips. "There is no wrong answer, honey," I say, hoping to put her at ease. "It's whatever you want it to be."

She doesn't hesitate. "It's an engagement ring."

I can't help smiling like an idiot at her pronouncement. "In that case...." I get down on one knee in front of her and take her left hand in both of mine. "Elizabeth Marie Jamison, will you marry me? Will you allow me the honor of becoming your husband?"

Tears spill down her cheeks. "Yes," she says in a shaky voice.

I pull her off the bench and into my lap, and we sit on the ground holding each other. I kiss her temple. "I promise to love, honor, cherish, and protect you for the rest of your life, and that includes vanquishing all your monsters."

"That sounds like a vow, Shane."

"Yes, it does. And you know I keep my vows."

She leans forward and kisses me, her soft lips trembling against mine. I can taste the salt of her tears, and I feel such an overwhelming sense of peace and rightness. There's a settling in my chest, like my heart has come home to roost. I'm home. She's my home. I remove the ring from the box and slip it onto her ring finger. She stares down at her hand, admiring the ring.

"Do you like it?" I ask her. "If you don't, we can exchange it for something—"

Beth throws her arms around my neck, smiling at me like I just hung the moon for her. "Are you kidding? I love it! It's perfect." She kisses me again. "You know me so well," she murmurs against my lips.

I deepen the kiss, despite the fact that we're out in public, starting to attract the stares of more than a few curious onlookers. I scoop her up in my arms and rise to sit back on the bench. We both laugh as we brush the sand off our shorts. Our small audience begins to dissipate.

I take hold of Beth's left hand, and we both eye the ring. It's just a tiny band of gold, with a small, perfect diamond nestled in the setting, and yet it symbolizes so much. I can't shake the fear that I'm rushing her, though, which would be a mistake. "Sweetheart, if this is too soon—"

She clutches my hand. "It's not," she says, tears in her eyes. "Shane, I love you. I want to spend the rest of my life with you."

I cradle the side of her face with my free hand, marveling at my own good fortune. Ironically, even though he's the bane of my existence, I owe Tyler more than I can ever repay. If it weren't for him, I never would have met Beth. I am indebted to Tyler for that. I wouldn't be surprised if he now regrets his decision to hire my company to protect his sister. But at least we got the job done—Kline's no longer a threat to her. It was a promise I made, and a promise I kept.

Speaking of Kline, Beth and I haven't really talked about last night yet, and we need to. I rise to my feet and pull her up with me. We need somewhere quiet and private, where we can discuss what happened. And perhaps discuss the future, if she's ready for that. The penthouse isn't always the most private of places, but I do know of a place where we'll be guaranteed privacy.

"Let's go to my office apartment," I suggest. "We can talk there."

She looks wary. "Talk about what?"

"About Kline. And last night."

"Do we have to? I mean, what's done is done, right? What's there to talk about?"

"Actually, quite a bit," I say, taking her by the hand. Quite a bit.

Reconnecting

We catch an Uber ride to my office building. On the drive to my office building, I take a moment to send a quick text to Cooper. *She said yes.* He'll know what I'm talking about. He was with me when I bought the ring.

The place is pretty quiet on a Saturday, so we make it up to my floor without encountering many people. We enter my office and head straight for the locked door that leads to my private sanctuary at work—a small, one bedroom apartment. Once inside the apartment, I flip on the light switch. Then I remove my gun holster and hang it, with my handgun, on a wall hook.

"Make yourself comfortable," I say, steering her toward the sofa. "Can I get you anything to eat or drink?"

"No, thank you," she says, shaking her head.

I can tell she's uncomfortable, not wanting to face a discussion about what happened last night. I can't say that I blame her. Last night had to have been traumatic, and I'm sure she wants to put it behind her.

"Sit down, sweetheart."

She drops down onto the sofa, stiff and wary, and kicks off her sandals and tucks her legs up on the seat. Her hands are in her lap, clasped tightly. I walk over to the small bar across the room and pour us each a shot of whisky in small tumblers. I top hers off with a generous splash of Coke.

Wordlessly, I hand the glass to her. She peers up at me, looking resigned. Then she looks down at the glass in her hands and frowns. "I hate whisky," she says, swirling it around.

I laugh. "I know you do, but you might appreciate a little liquid courage right now."

"Do we have to do this?" Her gaze is still on her glass, but it's not the drink she's talking about. "It's done. I don't want to talk about it."

I knock back my shot of whisky and set the empty glass on the coffee table. Then I drop down on the sofa beside Beth, facing her, and take one of her hands in mine. We might as well get this over with. "I killed a man last night. We have to talk about that. I need to know you're okay with it."

She looks up at me in surprise. "That's what you're worried about? Are you kidding? You risked your life for me! You could have been hurt!"

"That wasn't likely, sweetheart."

She shakes her head. "It could have happened. Something could have gone wrong, and you might have gotten hurt, or Caroline, or Jake."

"Honey, we knew what we were doing. There wasn't any serious risk to me or to any of my people. Kline never had a chance. The minute he broke into your home, he was a dead man. And I'm the one who put a bullet in his brain. I need to know you're okay with that."

Her brow furrows. "Of course I'm okay with it." She reaches up and strokes my face. "Is that what you're afraid of? That I would ... what? Blame you? Be afraid of you?"

She studies my face for a long moment. "That's it, isn't it? You're afraid I'll think less of you for killing him. Shane, no."

Her thumb brushes across my cheek, and I close my eyes to savor the pleasure of her soft caress. Then I feel her warm lips touch mine, gently at first, then with more pressure. I honestly didn't bring her here for sex—I brought her here so we could talk about what happened with Kline. But when her lips tease mine apart and her tongue slips into my mouth, I latch on and begin gently sucking.

Her arms slip around my waist. "Shane."

There's a wealth of longing in her tone, and my body responds accordingly.

"I don't want to talk about last night. It's done. It's over. That monster is dead, and I'm glad you're the one who did it." She lifts up and places her lips against mine, gently teasing me with soft kisses. Her hands fist my shirt, and she pulls me closer.

Already my body's stirring to her touch, to the sound of her voice, the natural scent of her warm skin. I'm trying to do the right thing here, but honestly, she's swamping my senses and short-circuiting my brain. All I can think about now is getting her naked and in bed.

I rise and scoop her up into my arms, and she sighs, slipping her arms around my neck.

"I want you," she says, and that's all the encouragement I need.

* * *

It's a short walk down the hallway to the bedroom. I lay her on the bed and follow her down. We both kick off our shoes into the floor, and she pulls my mouth down to hers and kisses me.

I break our kiss and brush her hair back. "God, I love you." My chest feels tight and I swallow hard. It scares me sometimes, the intensity of my feelings for her.

Beth's eyes fill with tears, and she reaches up to brush my brow. "I love you too," she says, her voice little more than a whisper. She smiles at me. "How in the world did I ever get so lucky?"

I chuckle. "I'm the lucky one."

She gives me a tremulous smile, then slips one hand behind my neck and pulls me down for a kiss, her lips soft and open and eager. I've been trying to restrain myself around her all day. After what she went through last night, the last thing she needs is me pressing her for sex. But damn it, I'd give anything to be inside her right now, sinking deep into her wet, lush heat.

I allow myself the pleasure of losing myself in her kiss. I figure a little making out won't hurt, especially since she's instigating it. Maybe I was wrong in thinking she needed space. Maybe she wants this kind of connection between us right now—maybe she *needs* it too.

I let her take the lead, and she nudges my lips apart with her own. With a soft sigh, her tongue slips into my mouth and caresses mine, stroking gently. I groan at her touch, and she smiles as my dick swells in my shorts, expanding by the second and demanding more space than my clothing comfortably allows.

I shift my position to give my erection some space, and she takes advantage of my movements to roll me to my back. The next thing I know, she's leaning over me, pushing my shirt off my shoulders. I sit up and remove the garment, tossing it aside. Then she grabs the hem of my T-shirt and pulls it up and off me. All right then. Looks like we're doing this.

I lie back on the bed, enjoying the feel of her hands on my chest. Her fingers trace the outline of my muscles, and the pads of her thumbs brush the tips of my nipples, making them tighten with anticipation. Her teasing strokes send heated pleasure coursing down my body, from the roots of my hair straight down to my cock, which is already painfully hard.

She straddles my lap, then unbuttons her own shirt and tosses it aside. I watch, captivated, as she reaches behind her back to leisurely unhook her bra and let it slip oh-so-slowly off her perfect little breasts and down her slender arms to land on my bare chest.

"That's just cruel," I say, picking up the dainty, lace garment and laying it carefully aside. She chuckles.

The sight of her bare breasts steals my breath, and I reach up to cup them with reverence, molding my hands to them and brushing her velvety soft nipples with my thumbs. Instantly they pucker up into tight little rosebuds. I've never seen anything more beautiful than the sight of her naked breasts. I could stare at them for hours and still not get my fill.

Beth's hands come up to cover mine, and she presses my hands to her flesh, encouraging me to knead her breasts as she gently rocks herself on my erection. I swear I can feel her heat even through our clothing, and the anticipation is torturous.

"Clothes off," I say, reaching for the waistband of her shorts. The sooner I get her naked, the sooner I can get inside her.

She brushes my hands aside, grinning. "Not yet."

When she presses her cleft against my erection, pleasure burns through my entire body, from the roots of my hair, down my torso, straight to my cock, which is straining against my clothing. "Jesus, Beth! Are you trying to kill me?"

She looks down at me, her eyes bright with arousal. "I want you."

There's no hesitation in her voice, and I realize then that she doesn't need space from me. She needs a connection, she needs re-assurance that everything's okay between us. She needs *me*.

"Show me," I say, my voice sounding deep and rough. I rise up and gently remove the band holding her hair in a ponytail and let the long blond strands flow over her shoulders like a pale silk curtain. I'm filled with the exquisite scent of her hair, and I breathe in deeply, wanting to lose myself in it.

I lie back down and she leans close to resume kissing me, her lips soft and teasing. She's definitely trying to drive me crazy, and she's doing a hell of a good job of it. The girl's dangerous. Her tongue slips inside my mouth, hesitantly searching and stroking, jacking up my heart rate. I can feel the hot rush of blood surging through me.

When she sucks on my tongue, my entire body shudders and I can't resist pressing my erection into her, desperate for her to touch my cock. When she doesn't take the hint, I grab one of her hands and bring it to my aching dick, pressing her open hand against me. "Touch me!"

She smiles against my lips and hums a soft moan into my mouth, as her fingers trace the outline of my hard, thick length through my cargo shorts.

I buck into her again. "More. Harder."

She presses her cleft harder to my aching cock, teasing me with the feel of her damp heat, then she lifts herself to unzip my shorts. I groan at the momentary loss of her touch, but soon her cool fingers are slipping inside my boxers, wrapping themselves around me and squeezing gently. Dear God, that feels good. Her touch is electrifying.

"Harder, sweetheart! You won't hurt me."

She complies, tentatively at first, but I think she's encouraged by my groans, and her fingers tighten on me. It's exquisite torment to feel her fingers wrapped around me. When she strokes me, I shudder, swamped by the aching pleasure of her touch.

She scrambles off me then and pulls off her own shorts and underwear. Then she grabs hold of my shorts and boxers and draws them down my legs. I lift my hips to assist, and a moment later, we're both naked. Finally!

When she sidles up to me and straddles my hips, I realize she's going to ride me. My balls are already close to bursting, and I don't know how much more of this I can take. I have to clench my jaws to hold still. I watch her reach between her legs and touch herself. She watches me as she runs one finger along her cleft, testing her own wetness, and then she takes hold of my cock and rubs the head of it between her slick folds to lube me up. Damn. She's going to kill me long before this is over.

All I can say is thank God for birth control pills because nothing's going to come between us when she finally puts me inside her. She positions the tip of me at her entrance and slowly lowers herself onto me, gently pressing down. At first, there's a moment of sweet resistance, when her snug little opening refuses to let me in. She wriggles on me a bit, biting her lower lip in concentration, and then we both gasp when her body swallows the head of my cock, surrounding it in sweet, warm heat. Slowly, she sinks down on me.

"Fuck!" I fist the sheets and hold on for dear life, afraid that if I put my hands on her, I'll bruise her, so I grab the bedding instead. She's killing me here, and if the expression on her face is any indication, she's enjoying inflicting a little bit of sexual torment on me.

She lifts up slowly, and I feel my cock dragging along the hot, slick walls of her opening. When she sinks back down on me, a little easier this time, I have to grit my teeth in an effort to hold still. I want to thrust myself into her so badly, as deeply as I can, but she's not ready for that yet. She's still working on accommodating all of me. I take deep, regular breaths, trying to reign myself in.

She makes such a pretty picture sitting astride me, wearing nothing but my engagement ring. I reach up and cup a breast in each hand, my big palms enveloping her sweet little mounds. My thumbs tease her nipples, and I'm rewarded with sexy little sounds that make me even harder, as if that's humanly possible. She moans, throwing her head back as my thumbs tease her nipples into hard little buds.

I sit up and draw one of her nipples into my mouth, laving it with my tongue, swirling the little pebbled tip before sucking on it, and she grabs hold of my arms for dear life.

She's moving on me easier now that my cock is coated with her slick juices. I lie back on the bed and grit my teeth against coming too soon. I want this to last. I want to watch her ride me, watch her chase her own orgasm and explode before I allow myself to come. She closes her eyes and rocks on me, gently undulating her hips as she searches for the right angle.

"That's it, sweetheart," I tell her, my hands skimming up her thighs to clutch her hips, coaxing her to move. "Find your pleasure and take it."

She closes her eyes and her hands come down on my chest as she leans forward. She rides me so perfectly. I reach between her legs and tease her clit with the pad of my thumb, stroking and circling the little knot as she voices her pleasure. Her eyes are closed as she works herself on my rod. Her cheeks flush a pretty pink as she worries her lower lip. I know when she's found the right angle because she moans breathlessly. Her hands slide to my forearms and she holds me tightly as her sex tightens on my cock. She's getting close, I can tell from the way her sex tightens on me, squeezing me so perfectly. Throwing her head back, she cries out as her orgasm hits her.

She rides me through it, drawing out her pleasure. And when

she's finally coming down from the high, I sit up and enfold her in my arms, then gently roll us so that I'm on top. I take hold of one of her thighs and hitch her leg up high so that I can sink even more deeply inside her. I'm in so far now that the head of my cock hits her cervix, and she gasps. Hell, we both do. I huff out a deep breath and withdraw.

It's my turn to move now, and I savor the feel of her slick channel surrounding my dick as I slide in and out, picking up the pace. Her hands are on my chest, my biceps, my shoulders as she caresses me. She meets each and every thrust, and it doesn't take long before I feel my balls tighten and draw up. I'm so close. I want this to last, but it feels too damn good to hold out any longer. I finally give in to my body's demands and let my orgasm overtake me, erupting hotly into her welcoming body. As spurt after spurt of my seed fills her channel, I slow my thrusts and enjoy the feel of my come inside her, so hot and slick.

After my climax wanes, I slowly pull out of her and collapse beside her. My chest heaves as I try to catch my breath. We lie like that for awhile, simply holding each other, both of us breathing hard. I lift her left hand and study the ring on her finger. *My engagement ring.* She's wearing my ring. It's the first step to making her officially mine forever.

I bring her ring finger to my lips and kiss it. "I'm going to be your husband," I say.

She smiles. "I can't wait."

"When?"

Her eyes widen. "When what?"

"When can we be married?"

Her smile falters. "I haven't thought that far yet. When were you thinking?"

"How about today?"

She glances out the window at the graying sky. "I think it's too late to get married today. Besides, I'm pretty sure some planning has to go into it. You know, licenses and that sort of thing."

"Okay, just tell me when," I say, climbing out of bed and scooping a squealing Beth up into my arms.

I carry her into the bathroom, and we take a long, leisurely shower, taking turns soaping each other from head to toe. When we're done showering, I sit on the counter with a towel wrapped around my hips and watch her comb her hair and blow it dry.

When we finally head back to the bedroom to get dressed, my phone chimes with an incoming call.

Beth picks it up and reads the caller ID, then hands me the phone. "It's Cooper."

I answer the call. "Yeah, buddy?"

"Where are you?" he says.

"We're at the office building, in the apartment."

"Can you come home soon?"

"Why? What's up?"

"You just need to come home. It's nothing to worry about, but I need you here. Both of you."

"All right. We're on our way. We'll be there in about half an hour."

"Perfect."

I end the call and toss my phone onto the bed. "Let's get dressed and head home. Something's up, but Cooper wouldn't say what."

I call for another Uber ride, and we finish drying off and dress quickly, then let ourselves out of the apartment and out of the building. Our ride is waiting outside the main doors when we arrive, and we head home.

Unexpected

What do you think is wrong?" Beth says as the driver pulls up to the front entrance of our building. She's staring out her window at the steady stream of people coming and going through the front lobby glass doors.

I hand the driver cash. "Thanks for the ride," I tell her.

Beth's hand lies frozen on the door handle. She looks back at me and whispers so that the driver won't hear. "What if they're pressing new charges?"

I reach for her other hand and give it a squeeze. "Honey, I don't think it's that. Cooper would have warned me if there was a problem. Let's just go in and find out, okay?"

She scans the parking lot and her gaze lights on Tyler's black pickup, which is parked near the building. I can tell the instant she spots it because her entire body tenses. I had already noticed it the instant we pulled into the parking lot.

"That's Tyler's truck," she says.

"Please don't jump to conclusions. Maybe he just stopped by to see how you're doing."

Beth shakes her head. "He never shows up unannounced. He would have called me first."

She's right. If he was here to see his sister, Tyler would have called Beth and arranged to pick her up in the lobby rather than risk coming up to the penthouse and chance running into me. Something's got to give. This animosity between us can't keep going on like this—it's hurting Beth. It's time for me to have it out with him once and for all.

I reach past Beth and open the car door. "Let's go in, sweetheart. Sitting out here isn't going to accomplish anything."

Beth is clearly nervous as we walk through the front lobby to the private elevator that services the penthouse. She's silent once we're inside and the car starts moving.

"Come here," I say, pulling her into my arms. Her arms slip around my waist and she leans into me. I kiss the top of her head and hold her close. I don't think she's as over last night as she claims to be.

We step out of the elevator into an empty and quiet unlit foyer. I was half expecting Cooper to greet us at the elevator, as he often does when he knows we're on our way up.

"Lights on," I say, and the chandelier switches on as we head for the door that will take us into the great room. Cooper's leaning against the back of one of the sofas, his legs crossed at the ankles, arms crossed over his chest. He's fairly radiating energy, so I know something's up.

"Glad you could make it," he says, pushing away from the sofa. He winks at Beth, and I know whatever it is, it's fine. "Follow me."

Cooper heads down the hallway to the rec room, of all places. He pauses at the rec room door, and I raise an eyebrow when he looks at me. I see a hint of a grin on his face, and that puts me at ease. There's no arresting police force on the other side of the door.

Cooper turns the doorknob and pushes the door open wide. Then he steps back and motions for us to proceed him into the dark room.

As we step inside, the lights come on and we're greeted with a raucous shout of "Surprise!" from a room full of familiar faces.

Cooper slaps me on the back. "Congratulations, old man!" he says, as he holds up Beth's left hand and nods at her engagement ring.

I raise an eyebrow at him. "You're calling *me* old? Really?"

Cooper grins, then sidesteps me to pull a blushing Beth into his arms. He squeezes her tightly. "Congratulations, honey. I know you'll be very happy."

A wave of friendly faces surges forward to shake my hand and hug Beth. All of my brothers are here, my sisters Sophie and Lia, Beth's mom Ingrid, my friend Peter Capelli, Peter's sister Gina, Beth's friend Gabrielle, Sam, Mack and Erin from the bookstore, and an assortment of friends and colleagues from work—Miguel, Caroline, Killian, and Cameron.

And across the room, seated alone at the bar as he nurses a bottle of beer, is Tyler Jamison—just the man I need to see.

* * *

An engagement party.

I didn't see it coming. When I texted Cooper to tell him Beth had accepted my proposal, he must have called everyone under the sun to put together this impromptu celebration. I'm sure he did it for Beth's sake. The man spoils her rotten.

"Thanks, man," I tell him, laying my hand on his shoulder. "She needs a bit of fun."

We're both watching Beth, who's standing in the center of a small crowd of people awaiting their turns to hug her. She's beaming as she shows off her engagement ring, and I don't think I've ever seen her happier.

"My pleasure," Cooper says, an indulgent smile on his face as he watches Sam sweep Beth up into his arms for a bear hug. "She's had a rough time of it lately. She needs a little happy."

As soon as Sam relinquishes Beth, my brother Jamie sweeps her up into his arms. Jamie's service dog, Gus, is practically bouncing on his feet, barking at all the excitement. Beth wriggles free of Jamie's hold and bends down to hug the dog.

Jake and Liam come up to congratulate me.

"Well played, bro," Liam says, a pleased smile on his face. "You lucked out. She's way too good for you."

I chuckle. "I know, thanks for reminding me."

Jake, stoic as always, shakes my hand. "I'm happy for you."

My sister Sophie comes up for a hug, followed by Lia.

"Congratulations, Shane," Sophie says, wrapping her arms around my neck. "She's a darling girl. Mom and Dad will be so thrilled when they finally get to meet her in person."

"At least you're making an honest woman out of her," Lia says, as she peels the wrapper from a chocolate cupcake with lavender icing and a tiny purple flower on top. I'm not sure, but I think the flower is real.

"There's food," Cooper says, pointing across the room at a table covered with hot and cold hors d'oeuvres. There's even a multi-tiered dessert stand filled with cupcakes. "You can thank Gina Capelli for the food."

"Gina put all this together on short notice? I'm impressed."

I stand on the sidelines and watch as Beth is passed from guest to guest, accepting all their good wishes and congratulations.

There's a commotion near the boxing ring, where Liam and Sam are facing off. They're both wearing boxing gloves and work-out shorts—and nothing else. Looks like a little friendly competition is in the works. Sam's good, but I have to give Liam the advantage here. He's a master of many forms of martial arts. Plus, he's a big guy, very muscular, with at least two inches and thirty pounds on Sam.

A crowd gathers around the ring to cheer the combatants on, including Beth. She and Sam have developed quite a close bond now that he's her daytime bodyguard at the bookstore.

"My money's on Liam," I murmur to Cooper.

"I'll take that bet," Cooper says, eyeing the two fighters in the ring. "Hundred bucks?"

"You're on."

As in all our friendly sparring, the objective is to pin one's opponent to the mat. Krav Maga and bloodshed are strictly prohibited. Other than that, there aren't any rules.

While Liam and Sam go at it, using a mixture of martial arts and kickboxing, with a little street fighting thrown in for good measure, I head over to the bar, where Detective Jamison is seated. Now's as good a time as any to get this over with.

Troy Spencer, who's acting as our volunteer bartender this evening, hands me a chilled bottle of beer.

I take the empty stool next to Tyler's. "Hello, Tyler."

He glances at me briefly out of the corner of his eye. "Shane."

We have the bar pretty much to ourselves since nearly everyone in the room has migrated over to the boxing ring to watch the theatrics.

"I'm marrying Beth, which means I'm here to stay. You and I need to come to terms with each other once and for all. This hostility is only hurting Beth, and neither one of us wants that."

Tyler sips his beer, then nods, but he doesn't look at me. "Agreed."

I lay my hand on his shoulder, which is tense as hell. He's so rigid, so unbending. No wonder he's still single. I don't know any woman who could put up with him. "Look, man, I understand how you feel. You practically raised Beth—she's like a daughter to you, and you want the best for her. I get that. I want the best for her too. As it turns out, she's decided that's me. I'm not trying to take your place. I just want my own place in her life. I'm going to be her *husband*, and all that entails. But it doesn't take away from your role in her life. She loves you dearly—you know that. But every time you give me grief, you're hurting *her*, not me. There's *nothing* you can do to hurt me, but you can hurt her. Is that really what you want?"

He finally turns to face me, his jaw clenched tightly and his brow furrowed. He must have come here straight from work, because he's got his Men-in-Black suit on, as usual. I get guys like Tyler. He's all about control, control of himself, his environment, and those he considers *his*. But Beth isn't his anymore. She's *mine*. That's the bottom line.

I decide to put this into the most basic terms. "She's *mine* now, Tyler. Mine to love, mine to protect. Got it?"

His eyes narrow, but he doesn't say anything.

"You can just sit back and be the adoring big brother now, okay?" I tell him. "Time for you to stand down."

Beth appears behind Tyler and wraps her arms around his waist, leaning into him. She's laughing at something. "Hey, Tyler!" she says, kissing his cheek. "I'm so glad you came."

Tyler swivels on his barstool to face her and wraps her in his arms. He kisses her forehead, his lips lingering just a second longer than necessary, and his eyes close tightly. Then he pulls back with a warm smile on his face. "Are you kidding?" he says, ruffling her hair. "My little sister is engaged to be married. I wouldn't miss this for the world."

The smile she gives him is beatific, and I know she's over the moon to have his blessings. I stand as Ingrid walks up and puts her arms around both of her children, and the three of them have a quiet moment together as Ingrid murmurs something privately.

It's too bad that Beth's father isn't alive. He'd be so proud of both of his kids.

Ingrid lifts her head and gives me a warm smile. "Hello, Shane. I was thrilled when Cooper called with the news of your engagement. There's no one I'd rather have as a son-in-law. Welcome to the family, dear."

"Thank you, Ingrid." Unlike her son, Ingrid Jamison has always been open with her acceptance and affection.

Lia pops up beside us holding her phone up to my face. "Say 'hi' to Mom and Dad," she says.

I see my parents' beaming faces on the screen of my sister's phone.

"Oh, my God, honey!" my mom squeals, her hands pressed to her face. "I'm so happy! Congratulations, sweetheart!"

"Yeah, congratulations, son," my dad says from over my mom's shoulder.

"Where's Beth?" Mom says. "I want to talk to her."

Lia pivots and sticks her phone in Beth's face.

"Hi, Mrs. McIntyre, Mr. McIntyre!" Beth says. "How's Italy?"

"It's delicious, dear," my mom says. "But never mind that. I wanted to congratulate you on your engagement to my darling boy. Show me the ring!"

Beth lifts her hand up to the phone, and my mom *ooh's* and *ahh's* over it.

"I can't wait to see it—and you—in person, you sweet girl," my mom says. "We'll be home for Christmas."

I'm glad my parents will be home soon. When I met Beth, they were on a year-long sabbatical to Italy, so they've never met her in person. They talk frequently over Skype or FaceTime, and my mom and Beth text each other daily, but they've never actually seen each other. It hasn't really hindered their friendship—my mother dotes on Beth—but I know Mom's eager to see Beth in the flesh. Eager to hug her, feed her, and generally spoil her.

Liam joins us, wearing a sweat-soaked T-shirt. "Hey, guys," he says to Lia's phone. "How's Italy?"

"Who won?" I ask him. "I have a hundred bucks riding on the outcome."

Liam shrugs. "Your money's safe. Jake called a tie."

Good. At least I'm not out a hundred bucks.

Liam glares at me. "Hey, which one of us did you bet on?"

I smack him on the back. "You, of course. You know I'd never bet against family."

"Damn right! Although, I have to admit, Sam's a pretty damn good fighter," Liam says, shaking his head with a begrudging grin on his face. "The guy's vicious."

"Good," I say, since he's Beth's daytime bodyguard.

"You're up next, bro," Liam says, clapping me on the shoulder. "In the ring you go. Show 'em how it's done."

"Me?"

"Yes, you."

"Who am I fighting?"

"How about me?" Tyler says, sliding off his barstool to stand in front of me. "How about a rematch? This may be the last chance I get to knock you on your ass."

Hell, yes, I'm up for a rematch. At least this time he can't have me hauled off to jail. "You're on, pal."

A Friendly Match

A re you sure this is a good idea?" Beth says, following me into the locker room. She grabs my arm. "I really don't think you two should be fighting... again."

I smile at her. "Don't worry, sweetheart. This is all in fun."

"Fun? You call beating each other up fun? Look at *him*!"

Beth points at Sam, who's sitting on a bench grimacing as he leans down to fasten his boots. He's wearing jeans, socks, and nothing else at the moment. It looks like he had a quick shower after his bout with Liam as his hair is damp. He has the beginnings of several bruises on his face and a cut lip.

Cooper comes around a corner with a damp towel tossed over his shoulder and holding a T-shirt. "Here, put your shirt on," he says gruffly, handing the shirt to Sam.

Cooper glances at us with an inscrutable expression. "It was a toss-up," he says, looking far from happy. "Looks like we can both keep our money."

But I don't think it's the bet that has Cooper in such a bad mood. I think it's the young man sitting on the bench, looking more than a bit battered and bruised. But why Cooper's so pissed, I'm not exactly sure, although I have my suspicions.

Beth follows me to my locker, where I store work-out clothes and my boxing gloves. She watches me change, her arms crossed over her chest, clearly irritated.

"Look," I tell her, hoping to alleviate her worries. "Your brother and I had a talk. We're good, I promise. No more hostilities."

"You think *fighting* isn't hostile?" she says, clearly miffed.

"We're not fighting, we're sparring. There's a difference."

"Yeah," my brother Jake says, chuckling as he walks up to my locker. "This is recreational. Tyler can't sic the police on Shane this time."

Beth scowls at Jake. "Don't encourage either of them, please," she says to my brother. "Where is Tyler, anyway?"

Jake points across the room. "He's getting dressed in one of the changing rooms. Liam loaned him something to wear. He'll be out in a minute."

As she turns to walk away, clearly unhappy about this rematch, I reach out to snag her wrist and pull her back to me. "Help me put my gloves on?"

She gives me a dirty look, but then she relents. I hand her a glove and hold out my hand to her, and she slips the glove on and secures it tightly with Velcro straps. I lean forward and sneak in a kiss, grinning at her. "Smile, sweetheart."

She fights a grin as she helps me with my other glove. After she's done, I put my arms around her and draw her close. "This will be a good bonding experience for me and Tyler," I say. "We've got to start somewhere, right?"

She looks skeptical, but she nods anyway. "Just be careful. He knows how to fight. He's been training in martial arts as long as I can remember. Whatever you do, don't hurt him. And for God's sake, don't you dare let him hurt you."

I laugh. "Yes, ma'am. I promise."

She rolls her eyes at me, so I kiss her again.

As she walks away, her spine stiff, I have a feeling Tyler's in for a lecture too.

* * *

Beth wasn't kidding when she said her brother knows how to fight. He lands an uppercut to my jaw that practically snaps my head off. We're boxing, just good old-fashioned, pummel-your-opponent-until-he-drops boxing. Some wise ass put Justin Timberlake's TKO on the sound system, and the beat is pounding loudly through the speakers. Yeah, Tyler's definitely going for a knockout, but he's sure as hell not going to get one from me. I'd never live it down if I let my soon-to-be brother-in-law knock me out cold in front of my fiancée.

I bite back a grin because I'm actually enjoying myself. Despite the fact I've restrained myself, I've gotten a couple of good blows in, even once knocking him on his ass. It feels good to get a little bit of payback at the guy who got me arrested the night before.

I spare a split second to glance at Beth, who's standing ringside along with everyone else. She's got Sam on one side of her and Gina Capelli on the other. I notice quite a bit of cash changing hands among the onlookers, but at least they're being discreet. I wouldn't want Beth to know that some of our friends and co-workers are either betting against me or against her brother.

The fighting gets intense, and Cooper climbs into the ring to act as referee. Apparently, he thinks we need one. There's a lot of boisterous cheering from the sidelines as Tyler and I dance around each other, taking turns delivering cuts and crosses and jabs. I've taken a few blows to my abdomen and given some as well. He got me in the jaw a couple of times early on, which was my fault for underestimating his fighting abilities. He's not bad for a cop.

My heart is pounding, and sweat is pouring down my face, getting in my eyes and blinding me. Tyler's in no better shape, and I think we're both too stubborn to concede to the other.

I finally get Tyler penned into the corner against the ropes and am hammering his torso, but he's blocking me pretty well. Cooper blows the whistle and hauls me back. Jake wipes the sweat off my face with a small towel, then shoves a bottle of water against my lips. A moment later, we're back at it.

It's obvious we're pretty evenly matched, and rather than let this go on all night, Cooper uses his referee card to eventually call it a draw. Both of us breathing hard, Tyler and I bump gloves. Cooper helps Tyler remove his gloves, while I walk over to where Beth is standing at the ropes, and she helps me remove mine.

"Congratulations," Beth says, smiling at me as she pulls the glove off my right hand. "You didn't lose."

"Of course, he didn't win, either," Lia says, pushing her way in between Beth and Sam.

I ignore my sister. "Of course I didn't lose. I never lose." I lean across the ropes and kiss Beth. "I'm going to take a shower. Go mingle with our guests. I'll join you in a few minutes."

* * *

After a quick shower, I return to my locker to dress. I hear someone in the shower room and figure it's Tyler. Sure enough, a few minutes later he's walking through the locker room with a towel around his lean waist, and he's toweling dry his short, dark hair.

"Good fight," I say to him, as he passes me.

He nods. "You too."

I finish dressing, then join him at his locker. He's fully dressed in his black suit and white shirt, seated at a bench as he puts on his shoes.

"See, that wasn't so hard," I say, patting him on the back. "We can play nice if we try."

Tyler glances up and smiles, but doesn't say anything. After he finishes tying the laces of his shiny black Oxfords, he stands and briskly tucks in his shirt.

"Thanks for coming tonight," I say, figuring it must have been hard for him to show up here after what happened between us last night. "It meant a lot to Beth."

He nods curtly. "I wouldn't have missed her engagement party."

"I'm glad."

I start for the door, but Tyler stops me with a hand on my arm.

"Shane, wait." He swallows hard. "I owe you an apology, for last night."

Based on the dark expression on his face, I can tell that wasn't easy for him to say. I shake my head. "Not necessary. We're good."

"No, really, I was out of line. Beth read me the riot act right before our bout in the ring. She's pretty mad at me."

"Really?"

"Yeah." Tyler breathes a heavy sigh. "You have to understand, when she was born my folks were thrilled to have a baby girl. They weren't expecting to have any more children. My mom had a really difficult delivery with me, and her doctor advised her not to have any more kids. Beth was... an accident. A *happy* accident, but still, she was unexpected. After she was born... well, my parents doted on her. She was a sweet baby, always happy, always smiling. She was so little and so perfect. I was a senior in high school already, but even I succumbed to her charms. Then my dad died in the line of duty before Beth was a year old. He was a cop, too."

Tyler stops speaking, dark shadows haunting his blue-green eyes—eyes just like Beth's. He shakes his head. "It wasn't fair. My dad had a beautiful baby girl at home, and he was taken from us far too soon. He never got a chance to watch her grow up, to know the amazing young woman she became. When he died, I was just on the verge of adulthood, and I felt it was my job to watch out for Beth, to protect her, like my dad would have. I had already moved out, finished college, and was already working as a street cop when she was abducted."

Tyler looks at me, his defenses down, and the bleakness in his gaze is painful to see. The guy blames himself for not protecting his sister.

"It wasn't your fault," I say, laying a hand on his shoulder and giving it a squeeze. "You had your own life to live. No one would have expected you to be there twenty-four seven."

His fingers come up to rub the furrows on his forehead. "I know that, rationally."

"I have younger siblings too, you know. I get it."

"I didn't just let Beth down, I let my folks down. I... failed them all. Especially my dad."

I reach out and clasp his arm. "You didn't fail anyone, Tyler. And don't forget, you were the first one to find her. I have no doubt you saved her life."

"Tyler?"

We both turn to see Beth standing inside the locker room, staring at her brother with sad eyes.

Tyler clears his throat, then pastes a smile on his face. "Hey, kiddo."

She goes to him, and he wraps her in his arms.

"It wasn't your fault," she says, her voice cracking. "It wasn't."

Tyler doesn't argue with his sister, but I have a feeling he'll never agree with her on that score.

She pulls back, looking up at him with teary eyes. "It wasn't. No one ever blamed you. Not me. Not Mom. No one."

He cups her chin. "Hey, this is your party. We're here to celebrate your engagement. No sad faces allowed."

"Come on," I say, clapping him on the back. "Let me buy you a drink."

Tyler nods at me. "That sounds good."

* * *

Troy breaks out bottles of chilled champagne, and everyone gathers at the bar for a toast. I can't think of a better way to kick off our engagement than being in the company of our family and best friends.

"To Beth and Shane," Tyler says, raising his glass of bubbly to a chorus of cheers. "May the future bring them nothing but joy."

Beth is beaming, and the sight of her so happy makes me happy. It's fitting that her brother is the one to offer us our first toast.

Tyler holds up his glass to me, and I tap it with mine. I think he's finally buried the hatchet.

Alone Again

The party lasts well into the wee hours of the night. By the time everyone has gone home, Beth is dead on her feet.

"To bed with you, young lady," I say, taking her by the hand and leading her to our suite.

We both get undressed and washed up, then fall exhausted into our bed. She rolls onto her side, and I spoon behind her, intertwining our legs and wrapping my arm around her waist.

She sighs and reaches for my hand, tucking it between her breasts. "Thank you for making nice with Tyler tonight. I'm sure it wasn't easy."

I kiss the back of her head, nuzzling behind her ear. When she shivers, I smile. "It was no trouble at all, sweetheart. I told you we'd work things out."

She brings my hand up to her lips and kisses my knuckles. "It was nice of Cooper to plan a party for us."

I lift her left hand to study her ring. "So, you think you're ready to get married?"

She laughs. "Yes."

I have to remind myself that she's only twenty-four. I'm a decade older than Beth. I'm ready to settle down—more than ready. I have been since I met her. "You're still pretty young, you know. If you're not sure—"

She turns her head to look back at me. "My mom was already married and had Tyler by the time she was my age."

"Yeah, well, that was a different era. Girls don't always settle down so young these days. Look at my sisters—they're all still single. Sophie's thirty-two and in no danger of getting married anytime soon. Neither is Hannah."

Beth brings my hand to her mouth and kisses my knuckles. "I'm ready."

It occurs to me that I'm the only serious relationship Beth's ever had. Before me, she dated that little prick Kevin Murphy for a short while, but that didn't end well. Kevin couldn't deal with her anxiety. She's had so little experience with men and with relationships. I don't want to box her in before she's ready.

She rolls to face me, brushing back my hair. "Hey, what's wrong?"

"Sometimes I forget how young you are, and how little experience you have."

"I know what I want, Shane," she says. "I know *whom* I want, and that's you. There's no doubt, no question in my mind at all."

Searching her face for any sign that she's not as ready as she claims, I realize I want to look at this face for the rest of my life. I want to be her husband—I want that claim on her. I want the right to protect her, to love her. I want a family with her. Kids? Jesus, we've never even talked about kids. "Beth?"

"Hmm?" she murmurs, moving closer so she can kiss the base of my throat.

"Have you ever thought about having kids? Is that something you want?"

She looks at me, surprised. "Of course I do."

I shrug, not wanting to make any assumptions. "Not every woman wants kids. Lots of couples are perfectly happy without children."

"Well, I do."

I smile. "I grew up in a crowded, noisy, chaotic household with seven kids, and I loved every minute of it. I want that for us too. Not necessarily seven kids, but a few at least. A little bit of noise and chaos sounds pretty good." I roll her to her back and hover over her. "And I know you'd make a fantastic mother."

She smiles. When we kiss, it's a slow, sensuous kiss

"About the wedding," I say.

"Yes?"

"Let's hire a wedding planner, and she can help you with everything. I'll leave all the planning and decisions up to you. You have *carte blanche* to plan whatever you want. Just tell me when and where to show up, and I'll be there. My only requirement is that I want my brothers and Cooper as my groomsmen. And we have to wait until my parents get home. How long does it take to plan a wedding, anyway?"

Beth shrugs. "I don't think it's something you can plan overnight."

"Well, the sooner, the better, as far as I'm concerned."

She chuckles. "You seem eager."

"I am." I grab her left hand. "I want a wedding ring on this hand. I want to proclaim to the world that you're mine."

She smacks me playfully on the shoulder as my mouth travels down to her breast. "You don't need a wedding ring to prove that, silly."

I throw off the covers and trail kisses down her body, past her belly button to the delectable spot between her legs. I settle myself comfortably because I plan to be here a while.

"What are you doing?" she asks, raising her head to watch me as I begin licking the hot, moist flesh between her legs.

I smile when she shivers. "What do you think I'm doing? I'm practicing for my wedding night."

Matchmaking

As I sit at my office desk Monday morning, I find myself fixated on my youngest sister. Lia looked like crap this morning when she came up to our apartment to pick up Beth for work. She's been struggling ever since she caught a glimpse of Logan Wintermeyer at my surprise birthday party at Rowdy's.

Of course we had no idea he'd show up there that night. It's a public place. Beth rented Rowdy's party room for our get-together with family and friends, but our group spilled out into the main area of the bar for drinks and to check the scores on the big flat screens. That's where we caught sight of Logan. Jake chased him out of there, threatening his life and limb, but not before Lia saw the little prick, so the damage was done.

Something has to give. Lia's been trapped in an emotional rut since she was sixteen years old. What that little prick did to her back in high school is inexcusable, no doubt. But still, for her own sake, she needs to move on. She needs to allow herself to have a healthy emotional relationship with someone. I know she's not celibate—but she never stays with one guy long enough for a relationship to even start. Just because her first boyfriend was an asshole doesn't mean all guys are. I think she just needs to meet the right guy—someone calm and steady, someone who's patient enough to get through to her and give her a reason for letting go of her angst and risking her heart again. Someone who's crazy about her.

I actually have someone in mind. One of our newest clients, Jonah Locke, might be just what she needs. He's a little bit older than Lia—he's twenty-eight, she's twenty-two—but that's probably a good thing. He's mature, and he has a calm, steady personality. Despite being a celebrity, he's actually a really nice guy. And best of all, I think he's a tad infatuated with my little sister. He met her once before, here in my office, and he's asked about her several times since then.

I have this crazy ass idea to throw the two of them together while Jonah's here in town to see what might happen between them. I discussed my idea with Beth and explained to her why I want to try this, and she was all for it. But it's going to require reassigning Beth to guard Jonah, and I don't know how well that's going to go over. Right now, Lia is Beth's driver. I have a feeling she won't take well to being reassigned. She and Beth are thick as thieves these days.

There's a knock at my open doorway, and I glance up to see Jonah. I met with him and his manager early this morning at their rental house in Lincoln Park to go over security measures there at the house, as well as Jonah's personal protection. I invited him to come to the office today to meet his new bodyguard.

"Jonah, come in!" I say, motioning to the chairs in front of my desk. "Take a seat."

Jonah's dressed casually in ripped jeans and an old, a faded T-shirt, and scuffed boots. His long hair's pulled back in a ponytail, and he's got more than a few piercings and black tattoos. He's a good looking guy—even I can admit that. He seems like the kind of guy who would appeal to a young woman with an attitude.

Jonah drops into one of the chairs in front of my desk, propping one booted foot on his knee. "So, what's the plan?"

I smile. "I want you to come with me. There's something I'd like to show you." Or, rather *someone*.

He stands. "Sure."

I escort Jonah down to the third floor, where the martial arts studio is located. My brother Liam runs the studio, teaching martial arts and boxing classes to employees and clients. Liam's won more martial arts championships than most people ever enter in a lifetime.

After exiting the third-floor elevators, I lead Jonah down the hallway to a large viewing window that overlooks the studio. Inside, the floors are gleaming hardwood, the walls are mirrored, and there are numerous workstations covered with floor mats and two boxing rings. Right now. Liam and two new recruits are standing on the mats in the center of the ring. Lia, dressed in black shorts and a matching sports bra, is seated on the sidelines, observing.

"So, what are we doing?" Jonah asks.

"Just watch. This is a demonstration for two new recruits."

A moment later, Lia gets up from her chair and approaches the mat. Liam and one of the recruits, a tall young male, step out of the way. Lia faces off with the other new recruit on the mat.

I glance at Jonah and find his gaze glued to the scene on the mat. "What's Lia going to do?"

"Lia's going to give them a demonstration on why they should never underestimate an opponent. Both Philip and Mateo are well versed in martial arts and combat. But I guarantee you, they'll take one look at Lia and think she's a pushover. Why not? She's petite, blond and cute. Surely she's no match for them, right? She's here to set them straight and teach them a lesson they'll never forget."

Jonah watches intently as Lia and Mateo face off. A moment later, Lia sends Mateo sailing over her shoulder, and he hits the mat hard. Mateo gets to his feet, laughing good naturedly.

"Holy shit," Jonah breathes, stepping closer to the glass. "Did you see that? She cut right through him. Hell, she didn't even break a sweat."

I smile. Yeah, he's a tad infatuated. "Watch."

The second new guy—Philip—is laughing his ass off at Mateo's expense. That's not going to bode well for him. He says a few things to Lia that we can't hear, but I see her expression darkening and her muscles tensing. Whatever he's saying, he's pissing her off. Not good. She's going to clobber him.

As Lia and Philip move into position on the mat and start posturing with each other, I sneak a glance at Jonah. Sure enough, his gaze is locked on Lia.

On his first attack pass, Philip goes the way of Mateo—right over Lia's shoulder. He gets up, and he's clearly pissed as hell. He mouths something to her, and then he makes another run for her. She reverts to a Krav Maga move—something totally inappropriate for this exercise—and renders Philip unconscious.

"Jesus, would you look at her," Jonah says. He's shaking his head in disbelief. "She's amazing."

Yeah, he's infatuated. "If you'll excuse me," I say, "I have to go chew my sister's ass off now for using excessive force."

"Don't be too hard on her, Shane," Jonah says. "I'm sure whatever the guy said to her, he deserved it."

"Meet me up in my office in twenty minutes, okay?"

Jonah nods. "Sure. I'll head down to the lobby and grab a coffee. See you in twenty."

As Jonah heads for the elevator, I shove open the door to the studio and walk in. "Lia! In my office! Now!"

She turns to face at me, looking a bit sheepish, and not one bit surprised. Yeah, she knew what she was doing. She knew she'd get in trouble for that move. I turn and walk out, managing not to break a smile until I'm out of sight. My little sister is a pistol, that's for sure. Let's see what happens when she finds herself spending some quality time with Jonah Locke.

* * *

That evening, after a very casual dinner party hosted at the penthouse, Lia leaves with Jonah Lock and his manager, Dwight Peterson. It took some doing, but Lia finally agreed to be reassigned as Jonah's personal bodyguard. She'll shadow him twenty-four-seven and protect him from overzealous fans and disreputable paparazzi.

And as for my attempts at matchmaking, we'll just have to wait and see what happens. Jonah's a good guy, and I'm hoping he can get through her protective walls and help her begin to heal.

It's been a whirlwind few days, and I hope that things are going to settle down now.

Beth and I head for our suite, tired after a long day of work and entertaining a rock star and his manager.

"What did you think of Jonah?" I ask her as we enter our private space.

She smiles. "My God, he's so gorgeous."

I chuckle. "Should I be worried?"

She shakes her head and smacks my shoulder playfully. "Of course not! He can't hold a candle to you, silly."

We head to the dressing room to change out of our dinner attire. "I see what you mean about Jonah seeming quite interested in Lia," Beth says, as I unzip her little black dress. "He couldn't keep his eyes off her."

"And he's a good guy," I say. "I think he'll be good for her."

Beth's dress falls to the floor, and I groan when I see what she's wearing underneath—a black lace lingerie set with garter belts and silk stockings.

Garters. Damn.

She knows what seeing her in garter belts does to me.

She turns to face me, a beguiling smile on her face. Yeah, she's up to something.

"Here, let me help you," she says, unbuttoning first my cuffs, then my shirt.

While she's busy unbuttoning my shirt, my gaze travels the length of her tall, slender body, stopping at the stocking clips holding up her silk hose. My dick starts throbbing as it fills with heat. Then my gaze drifts up to the front of her black lace panties, and dear God, I can see a tuft of blond curls through the lace.

I glance down at her, and I'm sure my gaze is as hot as my body feels right now. "You're trying to kill me, aren't you?"

She gives me an innocent look as she tosses my shirt in the laundry hamper. Then her cool, nimble fingers latch onto my leather belt, unbuckling it and pulling it slowly from my belt loops. Before I know it, my slacks are on the floor at my feet, and my erection is tenting the front of my boxers.

As her gaze settles on my cock, her cheeks flush a pretty pink and her breathing quickens. Her fingers go to the waistband of my boxers, and she licks her lips.

Jesus!

"Hold that thought," I say, sweeping her up into my arms.

The closet floors are hardwood, and I have a feeling I know where this is going. She's been practicing her oral skills lately, to my delight. But I want her to at least be comfortable. I carry her across our suite to the seating area in front of the fireplace and sit her down on the soft leather sofa.

"Do you want a drink?" I ask her.

She peers up at me, her blue-green eyes sheepish, and shakes her head. My God, she has no idea what she does to me. She's part sex kitten, part goddess, and the combination is enough to bring me to my knees. But right now, going by the flushed, eager expression on her face, I think she's the one planning to be on her knees.

"Well, I want one," I tell her, pouring myself a shot of whisky. I down the liquor, preparing to be tortured. "Lights, twenty-five percent," I say, dimming the lighting to a romantic level.

"Come sit down," she says, patting the cushion beside her.

As I do, she drifts down to the thick rug beneath us and kneels between my open legs. When she runs her hands up my thighs toward the waistband of my boxers, the heat builds, and my cock threatens to rip a hole in my underwear.

I tuck her silky hair behind her ear and marvel at how exquisite she is. It's not just her physical beauty that awes me. She's one of the kindest, most caring and most gentle people I've ever met. I don't know how I got so lucky.

She peers up at me beneath her thick lashes. "You're overdressed."

"I am?"

"Yes."

"What do you propose?"

She sits back on her heels. "Stand up and take off your boxers."

I can't help grinning. "You think that's a good idea?"

"I think that's a fantastic idea."

"Well, I certainly can't argue with that." I stand and shove my boxers to the floor, and she helps me step out of them. My straining erection lifts eagerly in the air, bobbing between us as it defies gravity.

She rises to her knees in front of me and takes my cock firmly into her hands, looking simultaneously apprehensive and determined. "I'm going to rock your world," she says.

I have to chuckle. "Sweetheart, you already do."

~ The End ~

... for now...

Thank You!

Thank you for reading Shane's novella! I hope you enjoyed this little glimpse into Shane's point of view. I hope you will take a moment to leave a quick review on your Amazon store for me. I'd be so incredibly grateful if you would. Just a few words to say whether you liked the book or not is all you need to do.

Stay tuned for more of Beth and Shane in *Shattered*, a full-length McIntyre Security novel! After that is *Imperfect*—Jamie's story.

Books by April Wilson

McIntyre Security, Inc. Bodyguard Series:

Vulnerable

Fearless

Shane (a novella)

Broken

Shattered

Imperfect

Ruined

Hostage

Redeemed

Marry Me (a novella)

Snowbound (a novella)

Regret

With This Ring (a novella)

Collateral Damage

A Tyler Jamison Novel:

Somebody to Love

Somebody to Hold

A British Billionaire Romance:

Charmed (co-written with Laura Riley)

Audiobooks by April Wilson

For links to my audiobooks, please visit my website:
www.aprilwilsonauthor.com/audiobooks

A Sneak Peak of Broken

Chapter 1

One of the perks of working in the security business is that I get paid to shoot guns and kick ass on a regular basis. I couldn't ask for a better job, and today's no exception. Later this morning, after I drop off my charge at her day job, I'll be heading to the company's private shooting range for my weekly mandatory practice. And later this afternoon, I'm scheduled to test the physical combat skills of two new recruits back at the office. We don't mess around at McIntyre Security—we keep our skills sharp. Plus, it's a lot of fun.

I've made it my mission in life to keep my skills sharp because, as the youngest of seven kids—the youngest *girl*, no less—I'm constantly being tested. Not so much by my two big sisters, but by my four hot-headed brothers, who are all pains in my ass. One of them—the eldest—also happens to be my boss, and he's got to be the biggest pain of them all.

My alarm clock goes off *again*, and I hit the snooze button for the umpteenth time. I'd really like to throw the damn thing across the room. I'm lying here trying to convince myself I don't have a hangover for the third day in a row, but I'm not making much progress. It's my own damn fault. I shouldn't have had those last three beers last night. I should have stopped way before that.

I've dallied so long in bed that I've only got thirty minutes to shower, dress and get upstairs to the penthouse apartment to pick up Beth and take her to work. Normally I don't cut it quite this close, but I knew this morning was going to be rough. I've been struggling more than usual lately, and that pisses me off. I don't want that asshat Logan Wintermeyer to have this much effect on my life six years after he fucked me over—literally. Damn it! After seeing him at my brother's birthday party a couple weeks ago, I've been reliving that nightmare like it's some perverted loop stuck in my head.

Every time I close my eyes, I see that damn video, like it's burned into my memory. I've tried to put it behind me, but I can't. I keep reliving the humiliation, the gut-wrenching sense of betrayal. I can see myself clear as day, losing my virginity to someone who turned out to be an asshole. Someone I thought I loved—someone I thought loved me too. I was so young and naive—*so stupid*! I deserve what happened. I deserved to be made into a viral laughingstock.

Feeling sick to my stomach, I haul my sorry ass out of bed with twenty-seven minutes to spare and stumble into the bathroom. My head's pounding and my mouth feels like it's stuffed with cotton. That's what I get for drinking too much last night. For the third night in a row, I came home after work and drank way too much—alone—in a futile attempt to forget about that damn video. It didn't work.

After I use the restroom, I strip off my T-shirt and underwear and step numbly into the shower. The water's scalding hot, but I don't mind. Even six years later, I'm still trying to wash away the sick memories of that night.

Closing my eyes, I lean into the spray, letting the hot water soak into my bones and muscles. I try to still my racing thoughts, telling myself it's in the past. What that bastard did to me doesn't define me. It doesn't make me less of a person. *He* was the asshole. But I've never had much luck. The memory eats away at my soul. Seeing myself like that, seeing the raw emotion on my face, knowing how he humiliated me afterward—it eats at me! He used that video against me, out of spite... God! I could kill him! I want to smash my fists into his face until my knuckles crack and bleed. And more than anything, I hate being unable to do a damn thing about it. I had my day in court, and I lost.

I slam my fist into the tile wall and choke back a cry as a jolt of pain streaks up my arm. I hate this! I hate feeling like this! After letting out one throat-ripping scream of frustration, I grab the shampoo bottle and take my anger out on my hair. But scrubbing my scalp until it hurts only makes my headache worse.

When I climb out of the shower and comb through my wet hair, I realize how long it's grown. I can't decide whether to cut it or just let it grow.

I guess I just don't care enough either way to make a decision.

* * *

When the private elevator deposits me in the foyer of my brother's penthouse apartment a few minutes later—at eight on the dot— I'm hit instantly with the aroma of freshly brewed coffee. That improves my entire morning. I need caffeine like I need air to breathe. I'd make it myself in my own apartment two floors down, but why bother when I know I can get a cup of the good stuff up here? My brother's roomie and right-hand man, Cooper, grinds his own freaking beans. Not me. I'm too impatient.

As I walk into the spacious kitchen, I'm faced with a whole lot of PDA. Beth's seated on a barstool at the breakfast counter, and my brother Shane is standing in front of her, right between her knees, leaning into her for some serious lip action. His hands cradle her face, and his lips are molded to hers as he practically inhales her.

They've had a rough few weeks. It wasn't that long ago that Shane shot and killed Howard Kline, the man who'd abducted Beth when she was just a child. After getting out of prison, Kline—the bastard— had decided to come after Beth to exact revenge for his two decades spent in prison. After her abduction, Beth lived under a cloud of fear and anxiety. Even though Kline hadn't had time to do much physical damage to Beth, the emotional damage was immeasurable.

Twenty years into his sentence, Kline was let out early for so-called good behavior. And that's how my brother met the love of his life—when her brother, Tyler Jamison, hired McIntyre Security to protect Beth. As they say, the rest is history. My brother took one look at Beth and he was a goner. She had him wrapped around her little finger in no time.

Beth seems to be recovering pretty well from the showdown with

Howard Kline. He came after her with the intention of killing her, but Shane was waiting for him, and he ended it once and for all, with a bullet to the guy's brain.

They've been through a lot. And I'm happy for them. I really am. Beth has an engagement ring on her finger now and she's deep in wedding planning mode. But still, it's way too early in the morning for me to deal with all this lovey-dovey crap, especially on an empty stomach. "Hey, Princess. Do you guys mind? Take it to your bedroom, will ya?"

Beth jumps, looking flushed and guilty as hell as she pulls back from Shane. "Oh! Hi, Lia!" she says breathlessly as she peers around Shane, trying to look innocent. Her smile falters a little, though, when she sees me. Yeah, I know I look like crap this morning. I have dark circles under my eyes. That's what drinking too much and getting just three hours of sleep will do to a person.

My brother glances back at me, annoyance written all over his face. "Yes, I mind. This is our home, Lia. If I want to kiss Beth, I will." He looks stern, but he doesn't fool me.

"You call that *kissing*? It looked to me like you were trying to swallow her whole."

He gives me a long suffering look. "My, aren't you funny this morning."

Naturally I ignore him and take a seat beside Beth at the breakfast counter.

They're both dressed for work, Shane in his white shirt and charcoal gray suit and tie—honestly I don't think he owns any other color suit—and Beth in a pale yellow, sleeveless fitted dress, her long blond hair drawn up into a carefree ponytail. As always, she looks effortlessly gorgeous. And so girly. Now that my blond hair's growing out, she and I look like we could almost pass for sisters. Actually, since she's marrying my brother, I guess we really will be sisters.

I'm surprised Shane's still here. He's an early riser, like before-the-crack-of-dawn-early, so he's usually long gone by the time I come up to get Beth. "Why are you still here?" I ask him. "Should you be at the office by now, bossing people around?"

"Good morning, sunshine," Cooper says, eyeing me from across the kitchen.

I hadn't even noticed Cooper over by the stove, which just proves how out of it I am this morning. Some bodyguard I am. I wave half-heartedly. "Hey, Coop."

Cooper pours a mug of coffee and hands it to me. "Looks like you got up on the wrong side of the bed this morning, kiddo."

"Don't call me that." At twenty-two, I may be the youngest person in the room, but I'm not a kid. I scowl at him, then take a sip of the hot black coffee and groan. Pure liquid gold. "Thanks, man."

"You're welcome." He hands me a plate of scrambled eggs, bacon and toast. "Maybe hot food will improve your disposition this morning."

"I'd better get going," Shane says, checking the time on his chunky Rolex watch. He pockets his keys and phone, then leans down to kiss Beth's forehead. "I'm meeting Jonah Locke and his manager at the house they rented in Lincoln Park."

Beth looks at me and grins conspiratorially. "Do you need any help? Lia and I could come with you."

Shane chuckles at her less-than-subtle offer. "Thanks, sweetheart, but I think I can handle one rock star on my own."

As he heads to the foyer, Shane pauses to look back at me. "I want you here for dinner tonight, Lia. Official business. Seven sharp."

I scowl at him. He knows I hate hobnobbing with clients. "Why me?"

"Just be here." And then he heads out the door and is gone.

"Jonah and his manager are coming for dinner tonight," Beth says, as I inhale my breakfast.

I met Jonah Locke briefly in Shane's office last week, and yeah, the guy's fucking hot. Like total sex-on-a-stick hot. Surprisingly, he seemed pretty chill for a rock star who makes the headlines every time he sneezes. "Why does Shane want me here? I'm not exactly the best dinner company."

Beth shrugs. "You'll have to ask him."

I swear Beth knows more than she's letting on, but before I can pry it out of her, she hops down from her seat and runs off to brush her teeth. The traitor.

* * *

I gulp my last swallow of coffee and set my mug down with a satisfied thunk. "Thanks for breakfast, Cooper."

He nods at me, and then stands there scrutinizing me as I rinse off my plate and cup and put them in the dishwasher.

He's staring, and that makes me uncomfortable. "What?"

He crosses his arms over his chest. "Nothing."

Liar.

"Did you get enough to eat?" he says.

Cooper's old enough to be my father, and half the time, he acts like he is. It pisses me off because I don't need another parent. I have two as it is, thank you, not to mention six siblings who think it's their God-given right to boss me around.

"Yes, *dad*."

"Don't get mouthy with me, young lady." He reaches out and grasps my shoulder before I can walk away. "You doing okay, kiddo? You've seemed off the past few days. Ever since Shane's party."

I shake him off. Cooper knows damn well I'm not all right, and he knows why. He saw Logan that night at Rowdy's, and he knows exactly what that asshat did to me. He's probably even seen the video, or at least part of it, and that skeeves me out. "I'm fine."

"Don't forget, you're due at the shooting range at nine-thirty. Don't be late."

I salute him. "Yes, sir!"

"Don't be a smart ass, young lady."

~ *BROKEN* is available in e-book and paperback. ~

Made in the USA
Coppell, TX
14 August 2023

20363709R00072